CHOCOLATE COVERED MISTLETOE

Samantha Baca

Stone Creek Series

Chocolate Covered Mistletoe

Candy Coated Promises

Pumpkin Spiced Possibilites

Contents

One
Brooke

"What in Sam Hill is that?!" I exclaimed as I shook my head and wiped my hands on the towel before tossing it to the counter, storming out of the bakery into the brisk winter air. A shiver ran through me as I marched across the gravel parking lot and stood below the workers who were hanging a new sign above what used to be the local flower shop. It had been across from my shop for years. I held my hand up, shielding my eyes from the sun that was beating down behind where they stood on their ladders, taking in the large, oversized sign.

"What do ya'll think you're doing? What is this?" I pointed to the sign as the two teenage boys looked dumbly at me as if they really needed to explain to me what a damn sign was. I rolled my eyes, reminding myself that I would need to explain to their mother, Sheila, that I'm not that stupid after they run home and tell her all about it. Sheila and I have been best friends since we were in diapers but that didn't mean that her teenage boys didn't gossip as easily as teenage girls at a slumber party.

"It's a sign, Ms. Hansen," Oliver shouted down to me, not realizing that he didn't have to yell that loud. I could hear him just fine from where I was.

"I can see that Ollie, but why are you putting it up?" I looked around, trying to find someone who had more information as to what was going on. My shop, *Sweet as Sugar*, was one of five in the little strip mall on Main Street and all of the shop owners had come to know each other over the years. If something was happening, we all knew about it. "Who told you to hang it up?" I asked as they pulled it up higher before mounting it to the wall. It was a black banner with gold fancy writing that said *Delectable Delicacies.*

"I did," a deep voice said behind me, startling me as I spun around to come face to face with the one and only person that I never wanted to see again in my life. Ryder Jones. I tilted my head up to see him, his brown hair showing natural highlights from the sun as his hazel eyes quickly traveled over the length of my body before meeting my eyes.

I forced myself to take a deep breath as I clenched and unclenched my fists that were balled up at my sides. I hadn't seen Ryder since he left Stone Creek, Tennessee ten years ago when he ventured off to Nashville to be with the so-called love of his life who was pursuing a singing career.

"What are you doing back?" I asked dryly.

"I came back because my father died," he said sadly, shoving his hands into his jean pockets as he rocked back on his heels.

"Yes, I am aware that he died. But you darted out of town faster than lightning after his funeral. None of us thought we would ever see you again after that."

"I had business to attend to in Nashville. But, now I'm back in Stone Creek. For good." He smiled his stupid, crooked smile, the dimples on both sides as prominent as I remembered.

"What's with the sign?" I nodded to where the boys had finished hanging the banner and were climbing down from their ladders to look at it.

"It's for my business. People might be confused if I keep the old sign up and don't sell any actual flowers," he arched an eyebrow and watched for my reaction.

"You're closing your dad's flower shop?" I asked as my mouth hung open in shock. "How could you do that?"

"It's simple really, I don't know a damn thing about flowers so I would be a terrible shop owner. My mom and I talked about it and decided it was best to let his legacy pass on with him," he explained casually, looking past me to see the sign. "Besides, I had a very successful business in Nashville that I think would do just as well here, so I'm using the space my dad left me and starting my own business."

"*Delectable Delicacies*? What exactly is your business?" I asked, knowing full well what he was going to say before he said it.

"It's a specialty shop with the finest sweets you've ever tasted. From cakes to truffles, I have something for everyone. I'll have to modify things a little bit but overall it will be the luxurious feel of a big city shop mixed in with the comfort of small-town living. A little slice of heaven, if you will."

"You cannot be serious," I snapped, shaking my head as the anger started to rise inside of me.

"Oh, I'm dead serious."

"You're going to open a bakery right across from mine? Are you out of your mind?" I shrieked, throwing my hands up in the air. "Don't you see how rude that is?!"

"It's business, Brooke, it's not like I planned to turn my life upside down and move back to Stone Creek just so I could make your life a living hell. I didn't ask to come back. I had a great life in Nashville with a business that was booming. I came back to take care of my mom because she's all that I have left, and I'm all that she has left. It was the right thing to do, which meant that I had to make sacrifices to what was best for all of us." He sucked in a deep breath and drug a hand through his hair as he looked away. "I'm sorry that my father died and left me his flower shop and that I have no desire to try to keep flowers alive. I'm not a bad person, Brooke. I'm just trying to make the best out of what I've been given. This isn't personal, it's simply business."

I worked my jaw back and forth as I glared at him and shook my head one last time before walking back to my shop. My momma always said that if I didn't have anything nice to say, I shouldn't say anything at all. Even though she stole it from *Bambi*, it still had been a valuable life lesson. Needless to say, I didn't plan on talking to Ryder anytime soon.

Two
Ryder

"Can you get all of that packed up and shipped over to the new location by this weekend?" I asked, making a note of when the last of my supplies would arrive on the pad in front of me. My best friend and former business partner had agreed to finish packing up everything that I wasn't able to bring with me before I moved back. It was a rush to get things closed down and finalized but luckily Parker was there to finish everything that I had to leave behind.

We had been business partners for ten years and had started the bakery in Nashville shortly after I moved there. He handled the business side of things while I handled the food side of things. I was scared shitless to start over again, this time on my own, but fate hadn't left me many options. If I wanted this business to continue to do well, I had better get my head out of my ass and learn from Parker while he was still willing to teach me. I wrapped up my phone call and scribbled down another date on the notepad before drawing circles around it several times.

My goal was to have a grand opening of the new bakery a few weeks before Christmas but that was already proving to be too tight of a schedule. The last few things from the other shop were scheduled to arrive by December 15th. That was a tentative date – and only three days away – not something I was willing to risk my reputation on. Instead, I decided to go with December 21st and prayed that I wouldn't be too late with people getting orders in for holiday parties and whatnot.

I glanced around the empty building, remembering days from my childhood when I would come to visit my dad and help out every now and then when he needed it. I wasn't much help other than when someone needed to pay for their bouquets but I still liked to pretend I was a valuable employee. I would stand in the middle of the room, looking around as I pictured myself being the owner someday and making my dad proud. I chuckled as I realized I was standing in the same spot, looking around, the proud new owner. Hopefully, my dad was smiling down on me from heaven and not cringing as he saw what I was trying to do.

The room was already filled with a handful of tables and chairs, the new tile floor already installed, and the display cases set up toward the back. Everything was starting to come together, slowly but surely. I still needed to paint the walls and hang up the wall decorations I had brought from the other store, but my mind was too busy to focus on any of that.

Instead, it was wrapped around thoughts of the fiery woman with icy blue eyes and chestnut brown hair that swayed across her back as her curvy little figure stalked off, giving me the coldest welcome home I had received so far. Granted, I probably deserved it after the way I had left things with Brooke before I went to Nashville but surely she couldn't still be holding a grudge against me this long… Could she?

My mom hadn't mentioned anything about Brooke's reaction to seeing me when I came back for the funeral but with how quickly her Alzheimer's was taking over, it was hard to know for sure. Very few people in town knew about it, my dad had constantly worked to keep it that way. The people of Stone Creek loved my mother and many had grown up with her, however, small-town gossip spreads quicker than a wildfire and my dad desperately wanted to spare my mom from taking the brunt of it.

Despite the rumors of me running off to the big city and abandoning my parents, I had kept in very close contact with them over the years. We started with weekly phone calls when I first moved to Nashville but as time went on, weeks turned into months and so on. My dad and I tried to talk as often as we could, especially once I knew my mom wasn't doing well. Nothing could have prepared me for my father having a massive heart attack but I was thankful that at least I had been given the opportunity to talk with him about what kind of care my mom was needing these days.

I glanced up at the clock, the only thing I had gotten around to hanging since I started moving stuff in yesterday. It was after two and I knew that the schools would be letting out soon, meaning that the majority of the kids would pass through the Sky View shopping center on their way. I wanted to get back into the swing of small-town living which meant that I needed to start making friends with those who mattered most. The kids.

My goal was to whip up a quick batch of cake pops that I could hand out as they walked by. It would be a nice treat for them on their way home and no doubt would create some buzz and excitement as they told their parents about them. The best business comes from word of mouth, and in this case—from kids who love sweets. I walked into the back kitchen area and let my shoulders fall when I saw the piles of supplies that still needed to be unpacked. There were a thousand things on my to-do list but right now I only cared about one. The cake pops.

After ten minutes of sorting through boxes and unpacking bags, I had the ingredients and utensils I needed except for the flour. I looked down at my watch and groaned when I saw that it was already getting late and I was surely going to miss my window if I didn't get started. The closest store in town that would have flour was at least fifteen minutes away, which would eat up thirty minutes just getting there and back. I let out a heavy sigh as I grabbed a measuring cup and slid my phone into my pocket, heading to the one place that I knew would have flour.

A bell chimed over my head as I opened the door to *Sweet As Sugar*. It was adorable inside with a welcoming vibe. There were a handful of booths scattered around the small room with a counter and display case in the back. The walls were lined with pictures of children eating sweets, which I had no doubt were the locals. Everything about the bakery screamed small-town and made me feel right at home.

A few seconds later a woman with blue hair piled in a messy knot on her head came around the corner and stopped in her tracks when she saw me. Her fair skin turned the slightest shade of pink as her mouth slightly parted open in surprise. I turned my head to the side for a second to suppress the chuckle as I watched her look over me like I was a giant piece of meat and she hadn't eaten in days.

"Hi, how can I help you?" she asked, her voice soft and overly flirty.

"Is Brooke here?" I returned the smile that she was still wearing as she glanced down and noticed the measuring cup in my hand. The flirty look she had been wearing was gone in a second as her eyes narrowed and her hands flew to her hips.

"You're that guy, aren't you? The hotshot, big city prick who is opening a bakery right across from us?" she sneered as she studied me. I could hear movement in the kitchen and hoped that Brooke would hear us talking and come out to save me.

I blew out a breath and let my shoulders relax as I offered her the cutest smile that I had, hoping she would put her fangs away.

"Hi, I'm Ryder Jones," I said, stepping closer and offering her my hand as I shifted the measuring cup to the other. She looked down at my hand then back up at me as she arched a pierced eyebrow.

"Oh, I know who you are. I've heard all about you and your fancy little chocolate shop over there. Whatever you're here for—we aren't interested." She glanced over her shoulder as the kitchen door swung open and Brooke walked out. She paused for a moment to look between us, trying to figure out what was going on. As quickly as she saw me, the look on her face turned into the anger I had seen on it not that long ago.

"What do you want?" she snapped, standing next to the blue-haired demon.

"Now is that really the southern way to greet a customer?" I teased, taking a step closer to her.

"Customer?" she asked as her eyebrows shot up high onto her forehead. "What exactly are you here to buy? Forgiveness?"

Ouch. Now that fucking hurt. I looked away, embarrassed, trying not to let her see the sting of what she said. I shook my head and decided this was a terrible idea. Why I had thought that Brooke would be anything like the girl I had left behind ten years ago was completely beyond me.

"You know what, never mind. Let's just forget that I came by." I pulled my mouth into a tight smile and bowed my head once at them before I turned to walk out.

"What did you come over for?" Her voice was suddenly gentler.

"Forget about it, it was nothing."

"Ryder…" she warned.

"I came to see if I could borrow flour. I wanted to make some quick cake pops to hand out to the kids as they walked home from school, but it's getting late and it's not that important anyway. Sorry for bothering you."

I lowered my head and turned to walk out, ignoring whatever it was she said before the door closed and drowned her out.

Three
Brooke

"I know we are supposed to hate the enemy, but damn is the enemy fine!" Autumn shrieked as we watched Ryder walk out and leave while I was in the middle of a sentence. I turned to look at her, giving her my best motherly look I had, given that I didn't have any kids.

"Really Autumn?" I tilted my head to the side and looked at her, annoyance filling every fiber of my being. The problem was that I wasn't actually annoyed with her, she was right— he was fine. I don't remember the last time I saw a man who looked as good as Ryder. But I didn't need her standing beside me, ogling over the way his jeans wrapped around his tight ass and how she was sure he could crack a walnut on his ripped abs. She was overly dramatic, to say the least, but now that she mentioned it, I wondered just how defined he was; his fitted t-shirt showing off his muscles he most like achieved effortlessly.

Life was just that way. Some of us had to work our asses off and were given average bodies with problem areas like thick thighs and an ass that consistently knocked over the bag of flour every time they turned around. I wasn't fat, but Lord knows that I was far from skinny. My mom always told me to embrace my curvy figure and that someday I would find a guy who would be anxious to take this body for a drive. The thought of it still made me blush to this day when I would think about her advice but she was never one to be shy about what she thought.

My mind had been circling back to the disappointment on Ryder's face when he said he was coming over to borrow some flour to make cake pops for the kids. It had warmed my heart that he would think to do something nice for the kids. When I first opened my bakery, I used to make sweet treats for the kids as well but as time went on and I got busier, it sort of just fell to the wayside and I stopped making time to do it. I glanced at the clock on the wall as I scooped a few cups of flour into a large bowl and walked over to Ryder's shop.

It didn't look like the door was locked, but I still didn't want to just barge on in. I knocked on the metal frame of the door and stepped back, looking around while I waited for him to come up front to answer it. A few minutes later there was still no sign of him. I knocked louder this time and stepped back when I saw him come out of the kitchen to answer the door. A faint smile crossed his face before it quickly disappeared.

"What's up?" he asked as if he had no idea why I was there. I lifted the bowl of flour and held it to him as if I was offering a baby Simba to him. He arched an eyebrow and looked down into the bowl, spying the contents before looking back at me with confusion on his face.

"You needed flour," I explained, nodding to the bowl. "So, I brought you some."

"Thank you, you didn't have to do that," he said, his tone almost curt.

"I know I didn't *have to*. I wanted to."

"Why?" He leaned against the door frame and tilted his head.

"I don't know?" I shrugged my shoulders, suddenly irritated with the conversation. "Can't somebody do something nice for you?"

"Nice? You want to talk about being nice?" His eyes widened with anger. "You have no idea what nice is if you think you're being nice. I appreciate the flour, really, but aside from that, you've been anything but nice."

I swallowed hard, having a flashback of a similar conversation not that long ago. One that shattered my heart into a million pieces and destroyed the friendship I thought we had. I lowered my head and thought about what to say, fighting the urge to hash out the problems that we never resolved when he left ten years ago.

"I'm sorry," I whispered, unable to say anything more. He nodded and clenched his jaw. I extended my hand closer to him, offering the bowl of flour as he reached out and took it. I turned and walked away, trying to force the toxic emotions from rising to the surface.

14

Four
Ryder

"Hey, ma, would you like mashed potatoes or baked potatoes with dinner tonight?" I called from the kitchen, hoping she could hear me over Wheel of Fortune. I waited a few more seconds then turned down the heat on the stove and tossed the spatula in the sink before walking around the corner to check on her.

She was sitting in my dad's old recliner, feet propped up as she curled under a heavy blanket that she had knitted when I was little. It was worn out and had been heavily used over the years, but I knew none of us would ever part with that blanket. She looked completely at peace as she stared at the tv, completely unaware that I was there. I quietly walked over to her and squatted down beside her, placing my hand gently on top of hers. She turned to look at me, her face lighting up the way it did every time she saw me since I'd been back.

"Oh, Walter, I didn't see you there," she said softly and patted my hand.

"Mom, it's me, Ryder" I whispered loud enough for her to hear as I tried to force the tears from my eyes. She looked at me with confusion etched on her face as she tried to make sense of what I was saying. I waited patiently for her to remember. Sometimes she did, sometimes she didn't and I would just go about, pretending to be my dad Walter if that's what she needed me to be.

"Yes, son, that is you," she said with a smile as she reached up and patted my cheek. I smiled beneath the fragile hands that were trembling with her touch.

"What kind of potatoes would you like for dinner tonight? I'm making fried chicken," I said, hoping she would stay with me long enough to decide.

"Whatever you want, dear, whatever you want." She smiled as she turned her attention back to the tv and I knew that I had lost her again. I walked back to the kitchen and filled a pot with hot water before setting it on the stove to boil. As I waited for the temperature to heat, I stood in front of the counter and planted my hands on the surface as I lowered my head and cried. Coming back hadn't been something that I would have ever expected to happen but now that I was here and really in the thick of things, I couldn't imagine how hard it must have been for my dad to have had to handle all of this on a daily basis. He had no help and on top of it, he kept my mom's illness a secret. My heart ached for the loss of my dad. I also had a great amount of guilt eating away at me for not coming back sooner to help him and spend time with my mom while she could still remember it. The tears ran down my face, leaving a hot trail behind them as I waited for the water to boil.

The nights were always the same and wrapped up early after dinner. I set a plate out for Ruby, my mom's childhood best friend, knowing that she would be by any minute. Ruby was a recent widow, having lost her husband a few months before my dad died. I had been told before I came back that she was one of the few people in town who knew about my mom and she had offered to come help me care for her after my dad died. She usually joined us for the dinners I made but tonight she had called to let me know that she was running late.

After dinner, she would help my mom into the shower and get her ready for bed. Even with the heart-shattering moments I had endured with my mom since I had been back, my favorite parts of the day were the evenings when Ruby would come over and they would sit and talk, reminiscing about old times and laughing at fond memories. My mom didn't always remember things from the past, but she still had a strong connection to Ruby and would find herself laughing at the stories as if it was the first time she heard it.

It was close to eight when Ruby came down the hall and plopped down on the couch across from me. I reached over and turned the tv down so we could talk.

"How was she tonight?" I asked.

"It seems like she's having a rough day today but I told her some of her favorite stories and she still laughed, so I'll take it as a win. She seems like she's wearing down some…" her voice trailed off and I swallowed hard as I looked away and focused on the infomercial on the tv.

"I'm sorry honey, I know you were hoping that it was better news," she said quietly, pulling my attention back to her. I nodded as I tried to force the emotions to simmer down.

"I miss her," I whispered, still unable to look at her for fear of her seeing the breakdown that was about to happen. "I should have come back sooner."

"We all have moments in life where we feel like we should have done something different, but you can't dwell on something that you can't change. What's done is done and all you can do is try harder with the opportunities you have left."

I forced a smile, knowing she was right.

"I heard a sweet man was handing out cake pops to the kids after school today," she said with a smile. I turned and looked at her, the pride in her face beaming through her smile. "That was awfully kind of you. Everyone is talking about it because the kids won't stop talking about it." She laughed and pointed a finger at me as if she knew that was my plan all along.

"Hey, I just wanted to do something nice for the kids. If it happened to get people talking about my new business, so be it," I shrugged and laughed when she tossed a throw pillow at me.

"Are you going to set up a booth for the Winter Fair in a few weeks?" she asked curiously.

"I don't think so," I said dismissively, as if I hadn't been thinking about it every time I saw a flyer slapped onto something all over town.

"Why not? It's the biggest event in Stone Creek. You know that" she chided. "You should set up a booth and let everyone get a taste of the delicious treats you make."

"I'm pretty sure Brooke will have her booth set up so there will be plenty of sweets already." I was making up excuses but the problem was that I didn't want to keep stepping on Brooke's toes since that's what she seemed to think I was doing since I had been back.

"Oh, Brooke…" she sighed and gave me a knowing look.

"What?" I threw my hands up and laughed, shaking my head as I tried to ignore the conversation that was about to happen.

"I've heard all about the heat flying around between the two of you since you've been back."

"Heat? More like I'm trying to walk through the fire she's breathing out the second she even sees me."

"I heard you gave her plenty of heat yourself if you know what I'm saying." She raised her eyebrows and wiggled them.

"Oh please, I seriously doubt that. She has not moved on from the past and is determined to make me pay for something that happened ten years ago. I was twenty-five and thought I was in love—can't we just agree that I was stupid and move on?"

"You were in *love* with her *best friend*. The only person that she had ever confided in that she had feelings for *you*. When she tried to talk to you, to tell you not to go, you blew her off and ignored her. Called her jealous when in reality, she was just trying to warn you that Lauren was cheating on you and had told Brooke about it. So yes, you were stupid," she laughed, "But you still owe her an apology for what you did."

I ran a hand down my face, feeling the prickly stubble that I needed to go shave. Yet another thing on my never-ending to-do list.

"Yeah, I know," I sighed and leaned back against the couch. "But how am I supposed to apologize when she shoots daggers at me the second she sees me?"

"Where there's a will, there's a way." She smiled and stood up, leaving me alone with too much to think about.

<u>Five</u>
Brooke

A few days had passed since I had talked to Ryder, things still feeling as awkward and uncomfortable as ever the few times we had seen each other. It felt strange having him back in town and running into him everywhere I went, even when I tried to avoid him. I knew that the market on Main Street was always busy on the weekends and that he would likely go by there to stock up on things for work, like flour, so I purposely avoided going until Monday morning when I knew he would be at the shop.

I couldn't shake the image of the kids flocking over to see him when they realized that he had cake pops for them, their smiling faces beaming from across the parking lot. It wasn't necessarily that I was surprised to see the kids that happy—you could give them a sticker and they would be just as excited. I was really touched by how happy Ryder had looked. He smiled down at them with the warmest look on his face as he passed the tray around for them to each take one. Butterflies had fluttered about in my stomach as I remembered the last time I had seen him that happy.

The market was relatively empty as I pushed my cart through the aisles, grabbing the few things that I needed for the week while looking at the stuff that I definitely didn't need. Like wine. Bottles and bottles of wine that lined the shelves and would look beautiful next to a warm fire with blankets spread out in front of it while Ryder and I made passionate love all night long. I felt my cheeks flush as I quickly sped past the display and tried to get the thoughts out of my head. As I turned the corner, I felt a jolt as my shopping cart collided with another.

My eyes slowly traveled up, finding the most beautiful hazel eyes staring back at me as our carts bounced off each other. If Ryder was as shocked to run into me as I was to run into him, he certainly didn't act like it. A tight smile pulled across his face as his knuckles turned white from gripping the handle of the cart while he watched me. I felt my heart racing in my chest, desperate to avoid him like I had been trying to do. I offered a quick smile before looking away and pulling my cart back so I could squeeze past him to get down the aisle.

As I started to push my cart past his, his hand reached over and grabbed onto mine, stopping it. I looked up at him, trying to figure out what the look in his eyes meant. It wasn't one I had seen before and it made me uneasy the longer he stayed silent and said nothing while holding onto the cart.

"I'm sorry, I didn't see you there," I said quietly, ready to take off the first chance I got.

"It's no big deal," he replied as his hand stayed firmly wrapped around the top of my cart.

"Well then, I better get going." I raised my eyebrows and nodded behind him, just in case he was confused about what I was trying to do.

"Actually, I was hoping to talk to you real quick." He let go of the cart and stepped to the side to let another customer pass by us, waiting until they had grabbed their bottle of wine and were on their way before he started talking again. "I wanted to say sorry," he said quietly.

I let out the breath I had been holding and waited for him to go on. It was nice of him to apologize but I had no idea why he was apologizing to me. When he stayed quiet for too long, I raised my eyebrows again and held my hand in the air as I shrugged my shoulders.

"If it's about us running into each other, I'm sorry too. Now can I go?" I asked with a sudden irritation in my voice.

He shook his head and drug a hand through his hair before locking eyes with me.

"I'm sorry for what happened when I left ten years ago, Brooke. I was young and stupid, and I should have listened to you when you tried to warn me about Lauren."

I felt the blood rush from my head, suddenly feeling dizzy as I never saw that one coming. Even though it had been a long time ago, it still hurt as if it had just happened yesterday. I could still remember the night that I bared my soul to him, begging him not to leave and trying to make him believe me that my so-called best friend wasn't the person who he thought she was. Growing up, I had two best-friends- Sheila and Lauren. We did everything together and were always inseparable. After high school, we stayed friends but each of us took a different path that ended up having an impact on our friendship. Sheila was the first to get married and start having babies at eighteen, while Lauren and I were nowhere ready for any sort of commitment.

When I found out that Ryder was in love with Lauren, it broke my heart. I had spent so many nights crying against her shoulder as I tried to figure out why he never saw me as more than a friend. In reality, it was that he was in love with someone else. Lauren had promised me that she would never allow anything to happen with Ryder because she was my sister and it was somewhere in the girl code that you don't get with a guy that one of your sisters likes.

Fast forward to a year later and I was standing outside, in the pouring rain, telling Ryder how much I loved him, as I broke his heart by telling him how unfaithful Lauren had been. They hadn't been dating long but if she said to jump, he would ask how high. It drove me crazy that he was willing to pack up his entire life and move to Nashville, not realizing that Lauren only wanted to go there because of another man. The guy that she had been having an affair with promised her a chance at the music career she had always wanted. Everyone in town laughed and looked the other way when she started telling them her plan. They all knew she couldn't sing for shit.

"Are you okay over there?" Ryder asked as he waved a hand in front of my face, pulling me out of the trance I was in. I nodded as I pulled in my bottom lip and chewed it, trying to force the recurring emotions to the side before I exploded in anger. Again.

"Yeah, I'm fine. But that was ten years ago so it doesn't matter at this point," I snapped as I grabbed onto the handle of the shopping cart and tried to push it forward before he reached out and stopped me again.

"It does matter because I can see that you're still upset about it," he said softly.

"If you didn't care about me being upset back then, why do you care now?" I turned and narrowed my eyes at him. His face softened as he flinched at the words.

"Because I made a lot of mistakes in the past few years and I'm trying to fix them. It may not be important to you but it's important to me. I want to try and fix things between us so we can move on and live in the same town without you constantly trying to hide from me."

I swallowed hard. How did he know that's what I had been doing?

"Fine, apology accepted," I said bitterly. "Now can I go?" I tilted my head to the side, trying to keep up the rough exterior so he wouldn't see how vulnerable I was feeling.

"You're the most stubborn person I know, you know that?"

"Yeah, well, I guess it's an upgrade from the jealous girl you left behind ten years ago." I arched an eyebrow as I watched his face fall before he let go of my cart and I pushed it past him.

I wrapped up the rest of my shopping and rushed out of the store into the blistering cold. I walked quickly, forcing a fake smile at the group of carolers who were huddled together by the entrance singing Silent Night. Christmas was less than ten days away and I had never been further from being in the holiday spirit.

<u>Six</u>
Ryder

Well, that didn't go as well as I had planned, I thought as I
stood in front of the cashier, watching the handful of sugary
items slide down the conveyor belt as she rang them up. A
few minutes later, she had tossed the last bag of powdered
sugar into the brown paper bag that was nearly bursting
at the seams. She turned back to the register and tapped
her long fingernail on the screen a couple of times before
turning to me and giving me the total. I nodded in agreement
and handed her my credit card.

"Someone has quite the sweet tooth," she said in a flirty
tone as she handed the card back to me and waited for
the transaction to finish processing. She was a pretty girl,
probably late teens or early twenties if that. Her blonde
hair was pulled up into a ponytail with side-swept bangs
that hung right above her chocolate-colored eyes. I glanced
at the bags that were lined up and waiting for me, bags of

sugar and chocolate peeking out of the tops of each one. I chuckled as I imagined how it must look to those who didn't know me yet and didn't know what I did for a living.

"I'm a chocolatier," I explained politely. Her brows pulled together in confusion as she thought about it.

"Is that like a three musketeer or something?" She pushed her lips out and crinkled her nose as if the thought of it grossed her out.

"No," I laughed at how young and let's be honest, ditzy, she was. "A chocolatier is someone who makes chocolates. I have a shop, just down the road, *Delectable Delicacies*." I smiled, hoping she had at least seen the new sign for it. She shrugged and shook her head as she waited for the receipt to finish printing before ripping it off and handing it to me.

"Haven't seen it but I'm sure someday you'll be just as popular as that Hershey guy," she said enthusiastically as she blew a bubble with the wad of gum in her mouth.

"Hershey guy?" I arched an eyebrow as I reached across and started loading the bags into the shopping cart to take out to my car. It was too cold to try to carry all four bags at once and honestly, I didn't trust them not to break given how full she had packed them.

"You know, the guy who makes kisses," she squealed before puckering her lips into a kiss.

I laughed and nodded my head as I grabbed the last bag and set it down in front of me.

"Hopefully someday I'll be just as popular," I teased as I smiled and walked away.

Ten minutes later I had pulled into the parking lot, the gravel crunching beneath my tires. It surprised me that they still had never gotten around to paving this damned parking lot after all of these years. I understood that Stone Creek was a small town but lord knows we weren't still living in the 1800s. I climbed out of my car and grabbed two bags, setting one on each hip as I carried them to the door and set them down. I went back and grabbed the other two, setting them down before unlocking and opening the door.

The warmth from inside greeted me as I pushed the door open and held it with my foot, reaching down to grab the first two bags. As I was bent over I heard a loud whistle over my shoulder as footsteps came up behind me. I stood up and turned around, making sure to keep the bags steady so I didn't drop them.

"Well aren't you a fine looking piece of ass in those tight jeans," Parker teased as he reached down and grabbed the other two bags for me. I laughed as we went inside and he helped me take them to the kitchen in the back. We set them down on the long metal island in the center and looked at each other.

"Did you come all the way down from Nashville just to check out my ass?" I asked as I wiggled my eyebrows suggestively at him.

"You know it," he chuckled. "Nashville is completely dried up with a real ass shortage since you left."

I had been unloading the bags when I suddenly stopped and looked at him, a hurt expression on my face.

"Wait—are you saying I have a fine ass, or that I was an ass?" I leaned forward and glared at him.

"You already know the answer to that one," he joked before ducking as I tossed the clean towel that was on the counter at his head. I finished unloading the bags and worked on getting the refrigerated items put away before they went bad.

"So, what are you really doing down here?" I asked, crossing my arms over my chest as I leaned against the counter behind me.

"What? Can't a business partner come down and check to make sure the other partner isn't fucking things up?"

I stayed silent, giving him a look, before he sighed, slumped his shoulders and leaned against the opposite counter, mimicking my stance.

"Alright, so maybe I thought you could use a friend down here while you try to get everything up and running. There's a lot going on with getting the new shop open, as well as you taking care of your mom. It's also the first Christmas without your dad so I just thought maybe you could use some support right now." He smiled warmly as his body relaxed.

"Thank you," I said, suddenly overwhelmed with emotion. "I really appreciate that." I tried to choke back the tears that were threatening to spill over. I wasn't the type of person that cried easily but after my dad died, everything in my world felt like it had fallen apart and tears seemed to be my new norm. I sucked in a deep breath and pushed off the counter, ready to change the subject.

"So, why don't I show you around and give you the official tour?" I said enthusiastically.

"There's more to this?" he teased, his eyes nearly bugging out of his head as he followed me.

He was right though, there wasn't much more to show him that he hadn't already seen. We'd spent a few minutes obsessing over the kitchen and how there was so much more space than we'd had in the shop in Nashville. Granted, there was quite a bit of construction that I had to do as soon as I decided to convert this place into a bakery instead of a flower shop. Overall I was happy with the new kitchen that we had created from the back storage area that my dad had used to store the flowers that weren't out on display.

By noon, we were getting ready to head out for lunch when I heard the sound of a big truck outside as they released the parking brake. We glanced out the door and I felt immediate relief when I saw that they were finally here to deliver the rest of the stuff that I had been waiting for from Nashville. Parker clapped me on the back and smiled as he said, "I told you it would get here in time," and walked outside to greet the driver.

I had been overly stressed, wondering when everything else would get here and if it would be in time for the grand opening this Saturday. They had originally promised to have it here by December 16th and I was thankful that they had delivered. Literally and figuratively. That left five days to get things cleaned, set up, and tested before I had to get busy prepping everything for the big day. An hour later, we waved as the driver pulled out of the parking lot and went on his way. I was feeling on top of the world with having

Parker in town as well as having the supplies I needed. As we were heading out the door for lunch, I grabbed the stack of flyers that I had printed for the grand opening and took them with us.

"Where do you want to eat?" I asked as I pulled the door shut and locked it behind me. Parker was looking around, checking out the few other shops around us. There were five shops in the tiny strip mall, all lined up to form a half-circle. My shop was on the corner, directly across from Brooke's, which sat squarely in the middle of everything else.. My eyes quickly wandered over to the sight of Brooke, bending over as she wrote an updated special on the sandwich board right outside the entrance to *Sweet As Sugar*. Last I had heard, she was only offering the typical bakery items- cakes, cookies, brownies, and a killer peach cobbler. But on her sign, she was advertising a new lunch special: grilled bacon and gouda cheese panini.

"That looks good," he said as he nodded in the general direction of Brooke's ass as she reached down to pick up the piece of chalk that she had dropped. Two perfectly round globes greeted us as she crouched lower, trying to catch the rolling piece of chalk that slid under a bistro table.

"It's a bakery," I deadpanned, trying to sound as uninterested as possible. "There are other places we can go eat." Which honestly, there weren't but I wasn't about to tell him that the other five options weren't nearly as good as what I imagined that panini would taste like. My mouth watered just thinking about it. I suddenly remembered seeing a large block of gouda cheese and a massive amount of bread in her cart this morning when I ran into her, which made sense now as to why she waited to go shopping until Monday morning. And here I thought it was just because she was avoiding me.

"It says they have a bacon and gouda panini, sounds like lunch food to me." He eyed me suspiciously.

"Fine," I sighed as I shoved my keys into my pocket. "If that's what you really want," I mumbled, as we started walking across the parking lot. Brooke grabbed the chalk before she stood up and turned around, surprise on her face when she saw us behind her. Her hand flew to her chest, forcing her to drop the chalk once again. I let out a soft laugh as I bent down and picked it up, handing it to her as I watched her look over Parker.

"Brooke, this is my friend, Parker. Parker, this is Brooke." I looked between the two of them as I introduced them.

"Nice to officially meet you, Brooke," he said as he extended his hand and side-eyed me. "I've heard a lot about you."

I rolled my eyes as I looked away, praying that he wasn't about to tell her about the drunken night that I had rambled on and on about her for hours after I had just moved to Nashville.

"Nice to meet you too," she smiled as she shook his hand. "I would say that I've heard a lot about you as well, but that would be a lie. Ryder didn't keep in touch with any of us little people after he left for the big city." She tilted her head to the side and smirked at me as I clenched my jaw in response. This woman sure had a way of getting my blood to boil despite the cold temperature as the snow started to fall again. It looked like we were going to have a white

Christmas after all if it kept coming down the way the local weatherman had predicted.

"Well, Ryder definitely didn't lie when he said you were a fireball," Parker shot back at her playfully. I watched as a blush flashed across her face before she glanced at me from the corner of her eye.

"So, what can I do for you?" she asked, turning her attention from Parker to me as she crossed her arms over her chest and shivered. My eyes were suddenly drawn to the sight of her cleavage under the knit sweater as she pushed her arms together to keep warm.

"We came for the lunch special," I said, nodding to the board beside us. She quickly looked down as if she had forgotten that she had one.

"Right!," she said excitedly. "Come on in and I'll get some going for you guys." She stepped to the side and pulled the door open, waiting for us to go inside. The smell that wafted out was an incredible mixture of spiced apples mixed with fresh bread and I wondered if she was baking the apple bread that she used to make when we were growing up. It sure smelled like it. We stepped inside as she followed us before making her way behind the counter.

"Did you both want the panini special?" she asked as she pulled out the notepad and pen from beside the register.

"That sounds good to me," Parker said with a smile.

"Same," I added in.

"Okay, I'll get those started. Do you want pasta salad or chips?"

"Chips?" I asked.

She puckered her lips and squinched up her nose before responding.

"It's a bag of kettle chips from the store. But the pasta salad is fresh, I just made it this morning," she said hurriedly as if she was embarrassed to offer us pre-packaged chips from the store.

"I'll do the pasta salad," Parker and I both said at once before laughing and walking over to take a seat at the booth by the window. I glanced back to the counter as Brooke wrote something down before going to the back to start our order.

"So, that's Brooke?" Parker said, pulling my attention away.

"That is Brooke," I sighed and looked out the window.

"How has it been with her since you've been back?"

"Fine, I guess," I shrugged and continued to avoid looking at him.

"Just fine?" He raised an eyebrow.

"Alright, it's been awful. She's still pissed about what happened when I left and has been shitty with me since I got back. I ran into her this morning and tried to apologize but she didn't seem to care, she just disregarded it and went on with her day."

He nodded and looked out the window which made me relieved that he wasn't going to keep pushing. We stayed quiet for a while, neither of us saying anything as we watched the snow fall peacefully outside. My head turned as I heard the kitchen door swing open, Brooke carrying a tray with our food on it. She carefully reached in front of us, setting our plates down before pulling her hand away.

"I'll bring you some water unless you want something else?" She looked between us as we eagerly shoved the hot sandwiches into our mouths, the aroma too good to wait. I held my hand up and shook my head to decline anything other than water as Parker did the same. She smiled as she watched us eat before she darted off to the back then came back with two glasses of ice water.

"This is delicious," Parker said as he covered his mouth with his hand while he finished chewing his bite. I nodded in agreement as I finished my bite.

"It really is, you've outdone yourself," I added before she whipped her head around to look at me. "Sorry, I mean, I haven't been around to know whether you've outdone yourself but this is probably the best panini I've ever eaten," I explained as I saw her face relax.

"Thank you, I'm glad you're both enjoying it," she said before she turned to walk away.

"Are you coming to our grand opening on Saturday?" Parker asked, stopping her in her tracks before she turned around. She looked between us, confused.

"I'm sorry, I don't know what you're talking about," she said with her eyes narrowed.

"*Delectable Delicacies* is having their official grand opening on Saturday and we would love for you to be there." Parker leaned back against the booth and smiled. I glared at him for a quick second before I felt Brooke's eyes shift to me as she turned to face me.

"I don't think I'll be able to make it, but thank you for the invite."

She looked between us, her lips pulled into a thin line before she turned and walked away. I tossed my napkin on the table and looked out of the window, too frustrated to look at Parker without reaching across the table and strangling him.

<u>Seven</u>
Brooke

"Howdy, howdy, who's ready to get rowdy?" Sheila yelled as she walked in, the bell above the door ringing behind her. I rolled my eyes and laughed, knowing that she was already up to something before she even made her way back to the kitchen. It didn't matter that there was a big sign plastered to the door that said: "employees only". As far as she was concerned, she was an employee. Or at least that's what she kept telling me. I finished icing the top of the cake I was working on when I heard her voice get louder as she greeted Autumn before swinging the door open and barging in.

"Well isn't that the cutest little Christmas cake I've ever seen?" she said as she walked over and bent down, taking in the details of the fondant I had spent all afternoon working on after Ryder and his friend left.

"Thanks," I sighed, taking a step back to look at it. It was all coming together just how I had pictured when I first agreed to do it. My back was starting to ache and my feet were killing me but according to the clock I only had forty-five minutes before Mrs. Crosby would be by to pick it up. "I just have a few more details to go and then I'll be done."

"Is this for Neil's retirement party tonight?" She turned to set her purse down on the empty counter behind me before hopping up to sit on it.

"Yeah, Mrs. Crosby will be by soon so I need to finish this before she gets here. Why are you all chipper, and what not?" I asked as I leaned forward and added another fondant leaf to the corner of the cake.

"I was about to head out to do some Christmas shopping and thought maybe my best friend in the WHOLE WIDE WORLD would want to go with me. We can drink hot chocolate and link our arms together as we go skipping from store to store singing Christmas carols." Her blue eyes lit up as she said it, immediately giving it away that she was up to something. I arched an eyebrow and waited. She blew out a breath and pulled the beanie off her head, letting her fiery red hair cascade down her back.

"Fine, I have to shop for the asshole and I don't want to be tempted to buy him laxatives for Christmas so I thought maybe you could go with me and we could find something together. You know, like a '*Merry Christmas you fucking piece of shit that knocked me up four times before you abandoned your family to chase your dreams of being a wannabe rock star*' kind of gift."

I laughed so hard that I snorted and had to turn away from the cake to avoid any unfortunate incidents. As dramatic as she was being, she wasn't that far off. Her ex-husband was a complete and total douchebag but she also should have learned that after he knocked her up the first time. In her defense, things had been good between them at the beginning but then they kept having kids one after another. Once they had four under four, he decided this wasn't the life he wanted.

She was a great mother and things were definitely easier for her now that the kids were in their teens but she definitely had a hell of a time raising them on her own when he first left. If it was me, I would bake him a cake filled with laxatives and watch the rat bastard suffer while shitting his brains out all day on Christmas. Maybe she was just a better person than I was.

"While I love your plan—and I do love it—I don't think it's going to work out that well."

She sighed and slouched her shoulders.

"Alright, what's wrong with it? Am I being too harsh? Should I be considering something nicer, or more Christmas-y, like pajamas?"

"No, it's not that at all," I assured her as I went back to work on the cake. "You just have some flawed expectations if you think that we can sing and skip while drinking hot chocolate. I've seen how clumsy you are—you'll fall and take me down with you and then I'll have to break up with you as my best friend because you made me spill my hot chocolate."

"And no one messes with your hot chocolate," she said before I could say it. We both laughed as I added the final touch to the cake and stepped back to look at it.

"What do you think?" I asked, knowing that it didn't matter if she didn't like it. After four hours, I was ready to call this cake what it was. Done.

She scooted forward and slid off the counter, coming to stand next to me as she admired it.

"It's really beautiful, you did a great job." She wrapped her arms around my shoulders and gave me a quick squeeze.

"Thanks," I said as I smiled at her and glanced at the clock hanging on the wall behind her. Ten minutes left but if I knew Mrs. Crosby, she would be here in five.

"Awesome, I'm going to run to the little girl's room while you get that packed up, then we can get out of here and do some shopping." She turned to walk into the employee bathroom in the back when she heard me groan at the idea of shopping. "You can't be a grinch forever. Maybe I'll find some mistletoe and attach it to a hat that you can wear around town until someone slips a present in your stocking if you know what I mean?" She winked dramatically as she said it.

"You're disgusting," I replied as I shook my head and turned my attention back to getting the cake boxed up. I heard the bathroom door close and was relieved that I had a few minutes to spare before I heard the bell ring up front as Mrs. Crosby came in. I closed the lid on the cake and taped the sides to make sure everything stayed secure before I picked it up and carried it out to the front.

Autumn smiled and squealed when she saw it, completely different from when she had seen it a few hours ago after I had just started to work on it. She went to the register and began to ring Mrs. Crosby up for me while they continued to talk about how beautiful the cake was. Her husband, Neil, was retiring after thirty years as the school crossing guard. I could still remember seeing him every day, helping the children cross the street as we went to and from school. Stone Creek wasn't very big and everyone in town was well aware of how to act in a school zone, or just being close to a school for that matter. But still, Mr. Crosby had taken the job and did it with pride every single day. I remembered him taking my small hand and helping me cross the street plenty of times when I was a little girl.

I was still lost in thought as I watched her walk out the door with the cake, excitement on her face. She carefully loaded it into the passenger side of her car before she hurried around to the other side to get in. The door from the kitchen swung open and Sheila came walking out with her purse already on one arm with mine hanging off the other.

"You ready to go?" she asked cheerfully?

I looked down at my flour and frosting covered apron then at her. She was wearing tight fitted jeans that wrapped perfectly around her petite frame and a white cashmere turtleneck sweater that hugged her perky, yet overly plump, breasts. A beautiful silver locket hung down between her cleavage, adding to the overall outfit that she had probably spent two minutes throwing together. She was naturally beautiful without trying, which always surprised me as to why she was still single. Not that the men in town hadn't tried. Sheila had been saying that she wasn't interested in a relationship ever since Rodney left her twelve years ago.

"I'm kind of a mess, I should at least go home and change first," I said, hoping she would change her mind about wanting to go.

"No need, I already stopped by your place and grabbed you something to change into. It's on your desk in the back, so go, get moving before the stores start to close and we don't get any shopping done." She nodded to the back and eyed me like I was one of her children until I gave in and walked back to find she had laid out a pair of jeans, my favorite sweater, and a pair of over the knee boots I had been wanting but refused to buy. I ran my hand along the soft leather and closed my eyes for a second to keep from crying. We had been out shopping together months ago when I had seen these and fell in love with them but couldn't afford them.

We had been out for a girls' weekend while her parents took her kids on a camping trip and decided to do some shopping in Clarksville which was an hour drive from Stone Creek and the stores were way more expensive than anything in our small town. The nice thing about shopping in a bigger city was that we could find things that we couldn't find at our teeny-tiny shops, and it was more of a treat to splurge on the finer things every now and then.

"We don't have all day, just put those sexy boots on your tired feet and let's get going," Sheila called from up front. I sighed and shook my head before slipping into the bathroom to change. I tossed my dirty clothes onto my desk and headed up front.

"I've got everything here, go and have fun," Autumn said as if sensing my reservations about leaving.

"You sure?" I raised an eyebrow.

"Yes, *mom*, I'm sure. I've already cleaned up and plan to close by five if we don't have anyone coming in to place any holiday orders. After that, I'll stick around to work on the supply list before I go."

"Okay, I'll have my phone on if you need me. See you in the morning." I smiled and walked out, knowing that Autumn was fully capable of handling everything on her own. I felt Sheila's arm slide into mine and laughed as we linked arms and started walking. I figured she wanted to check out the other stores in the shopping center first since they were the most popular but when she started to pull me in the opposite direction, I started to panic.

"Where are you going?" I asked as I tried to slow her down as she pulled harder.

"There is this new chocolate place that I HAVE TO TRY! Come on, I want to see if it's open yet," she squealed as we walked toward Ryder's shop. I stopped in my tracks and glared at her.

"You know damn well whose shop that is," I said, letting her arm drop as my hand planted itself on my hip.

"Yeah, and?"

"I've had enough of Ryder, I don't feel like going into his shop. If you want to go, you have to go by yourself. Besides, I think they said the grand opening is Saturday so I doubt that it's even open yet." I walked over and sat on the edge of the cement planter box that lined the edge of where the sidewalk bordered the parking lot. Her eyes widened as she listened to what I said.

"Oh really? And when did you talk to Ryder to find out about a grand opening?" she asked as she stepped closer and stood in front of me. Then suddenly it clicked and her eyes went even bigger. "Who are *they*?"

I blew out a frustrated breath and glanced over my shoulder at the shop.

"Ryder and his friend came by my shop today for lunch. His friend, Parker, asked if I was coming to the grand opening on Saturday."

"Who is this guy Parker? Is he single? Cute?" she scrunched her nose up and wrinkled her brows.

"I thought you weren't interested in dating anyone?" I teased and tried to change the subject.

"That was before I realized that WE are about to turn 35 and WE need to find men in our lives." She sat down next to me and nudged me with her shoulder.

"Why do WE have to do everything together? Can't your 35-year-old self go man-hunting on your own?"

"I could, but it would be more fun if we did it together. Then we can skip and drink wine while we compare horror stories of dates gone wrong while we wait for our Prince Charming to come along and rescue us," she said in a sing-song tone.

"Why are we always drinking and skipping? It seems like such a bad idea," I groaned. "Almost as bad as us dating."

She laughed and grabbed my arm, pulling me up as she dragged me with her to *Delectable Delicacies*.

Eight
Ryder

The afternoon had been quiet with Parker working on paperwork while I started unpacking everything that had come in this morning. Finally, an hour ago, it felt like the shop was set up and ready to go. I decided to get a head start on making some of my favorite holiday chocolates, to not only ensure that I really did have everything I needed but more importantly, that everything was working properly before Saturday's grand opening. This wasn't my first grand opening but even though I knew more than half of the people who would be there, I had never been this nervous or anxious starting my own shop in my life. Maybe it was all of the pressure I was putting on myself to take over my dad's shop and turn it into something he would be proud of.

I gently wiped the sides of the tray of chocolate-covered cashews and set them next to the trays of chocolate-covered peanuts and almonds. Everything was coming together smoothly and before I knew it, I had a display case full of chocolate-covered treats. I stepped back to admire my work when I heard the bell chime as the front door opened. I wasn't technically open yet, however, I also knew better than to turn anyone away in a small town. Plus it wouldn't hurt to sell some of the chocolates I had made while they were fresh.

My eyes narrowed as I tried to see who was coming in as the sun reflected off of the glass of the door, nearly blinding me. I needed to make a note to have that fixed as soon as possible. A few seconds later, I held my breath as I looked at the two women standing at the entrance. Brooke looked around nervously as she tugged on the sleeve of her sweater, obviously wishing she was anywhere but here right now. The sun caught her brown hair and cast a beautiful warm glow on it, reminding me just how gorgeous she was. My eyes slowly traveled over her body, admiring the way her jeans hugged every curve while taking note of the sexy boots she was wearing with them. I silently wished she would turn around so I could check out her plump ass in something other than the loose pants she's worn the past few times I've seen her.

It made sense not to wear tight or restrictive clothes when you were rushing around a kitchen like a mad man but now that I saw her in this, I never wanted her to wear her work clothes ever again. Maybe I could somehow convince her that it's a new trend to bake in jeans and a tight t-shirt, or maybe even nothing at all? I shook my head to try to get rid of the image before I embarrassed myself. That was something that I could save for later. A better time, a better place.

I had been so caught up checking Brooke out that I had spaced that there was someone else who had come in with her. I glanced up and saw Sheila walking over to me, a huge smile on her face. I returned her smile, genuinely happy to see her. She came running the last few steps and leaped into my arms as I wrapped her in a big hug and gently squeezed her.

"It's so good to have you back," she whispered as she pulled back and cupped my cheeks in her hands. "I'm so sorry about your dad, we all miss him so much."

I lifted my hands and gently squeezed hers while she still held onto my face.

"Thank you, it's good to be back. And I miss him too."

She smiled a sad smile as we slowly let go of each other's hands and stepped to the side. Brooke had finally walked over and was standing next to Sheila, glancing behind us toward the display case.

"Hey," I said as I nodded at Brooke, hoping things would be a little easier between us than they were earlier. I was still feeling frustrated with how things had been going but it seemed every time I made any effort with her, it was quickly rejected and ended up being all for nothing.

"Hi." Her eyes quickly met mine before she pulled away and stepped to the side to look at the chocolates in the case.

"You've been busy," she said as she bent forward and studied each piece.

"I had a little time on my hands this afternoon and wanted to make sure everything was up and running before the grand opening on Saturday," I explained as I saw Parker come out from the kitchen. He stopped in his tracks when he saw there were customers and was about to turn around and go back to the kitchen when he spotted Brooke. His eyes widened as he wiggled his eyebrows before noticing Sheila. As if having Brooke here wasn't enough of a reason for him to stay and make my life hell, he now found a new target and headed over.

"Is there anything that you don't cover in chocolate?" Brooke mumbled more as a statement than an actual question.

"I'm sure he's willing to experiment with body parts if the right woman came along," Parker teased as he walked over, forcing Brooke's head to whip up as she started to blush. I worked my jaw back and forth as I glared at him before turning my attention to Brooke. Her expression was priceless and no matter how much she tried to hide it, she looked like she was considering what he just said.

"I wouldn't know anything about that," Brooke said curtly before looking away from Parker and at me. She gave me the same look she had in her eyes the night everything between us changed after she had admitted that she was falling in love with me. Feeling bolder than usual and tired of the bullshit from the past, I decided to push back.

"I still have a few extra hours that I could spare if you're interested." I looked her dead in the eye and held her gaze as I raised my eyebrows and rocked back on my heels. I expected her to blush and look away like she always did but instead, she surprised me.

"I have better things to do than to mess with little boys who still play with their food." She tilted her head as she challenged me to respond, instead, I rolled my eyes and looked away. "Did you get what you came in here for?" She asked as she turned to Sheila and glared at her. I really got under her skin, that was apparent. Suddenly I had the urge to get even further beneath it, just to see how feisty she was these days.

"Actually, I needed to see about placing a holiday order for Christmas Eve. My ex-in-laws are coming to town and I promised the kids that we would have something nice for them."

I watched as she nervously looked at Parker who was still standing off to the side watching everything in silence. He was watching her intently and I was surprised when I didn't see him flinch when she mentioned former in-laws or kids. Maybe since he was older than me and turning forty this year, it didn't bother or surprise him to hear that a woman had been married and had kids.

"Yeah, we can get an order placed for you," I said as I noticed Brooke walking off toward the door to go outside. "Parker here will get you started." I clapped him on the back and smirked as I took off to the front after Brooke. I could hear his jaw drop to the floor when he realized that I had left him alone with a beautiful woman and he had no fucking idea what to do with placing an order for her. Maybe now he would understand that karma could bite you in the ass pretty quickly and he would stay out of things with Brooke.

I reached forward and grabbed the door before it could close and slid outside as Brooke was walking over to the bench that sat in front of the gift shop, separating our stores. She turned around and sat down, shivering against the cold chill, before she looked up and spotted me. She shook her head and scowled as she looked the other way. I turned around and sat down next to her, leaning forward to rest my elbows on my thighs as I looked out into the nearly empty parking lot.

"Why do you hate me so much?" I asked as I kept staring straight ahead. I felt her shift, scooting slightly away from me as she crossed her leg in the opposite direction.

"I don't hate you," she said softly, her arms crossed over her chest as her purse rested on her thigh.

"You sure seem like you do. There's a lot of anger whenever I try to talk to you." I slightly turned to look at her over my shoulder.

"Maybe I never really got over what happened." She shrugged.

"I can see that," I joked, immediately regretting it when her head turned and she glared at me. "I don't blame you though, I would have been angry too. And in all honesty, I should have listened to you."

"But you didn't."

"But I didn't," I sighed as I leaned back and rested against the cold wood of the bench. I had played that night over and over in my head so many times that I could recite each word that was said verbatim. It was one of those things that felt like they happened in slow motion and you knew that there was going to be a terrible outcome but yet there wasn't anything you could do to stop it other than watch in agony.

"I knew that Lauren was cheating on me," I admitted,

embarrassed. I felt the bench shift as she shifted and turned to look at me, a puzzled look on her face when we locked eyes.

"Then why didn't you tell me? Why did you let me go on and on, embarrassing myself as I begged you to stay?" The hurt in her voice felt like a knife plunging through to my chest. "Why did you still go with her?"

"Because," I took a deep breath, unsure of whether I was ready to say this out loud for the first time to anyone. "It was easier to move away with someone who didn't love me than it was to stay here and admit that I was falling in love with you."

I heard her gasp as she brought her hand to her chest and stared at me.

"What?" she whispered.

"I was falling in love with you, Brooke, but I didn't feel like I was allowed to. You were like my little sister when we were growing up, then you were one of my best friends. I didn't know how to handle it and I kept fighting what I was feeling. I wasn't going to move to Nashville with Lauren but then you said you were falling in love with me and I got scared… So I went so that I could keep from hurting you." I tried to swallow down the emotion that was bubbling up, forcing myself not to lose it in front of her.

"You hurt me even more with what you did. You left *AFTER* I told you I had feelings for you, and you left with my best friend who was cheating on you." She shook her head and turned to the side, her fingers trembling as she wiped a tear away as it slid down her cheek.

"I know and I'm so sorry. I will never stop apologizing for what I did." I turned to look at her, reaching over to gently touch her chin as I tried to get her to look at me. Her eyes were filled with tears as her lip trembled. "I was young and stupid, nothing will ever change that. But I knew the moment I left that I had made a *HUGE* mistake. The only reason that I didn't come back to fix it was because I thought you deserved someone better than that. Someone who would know better than to hurt you like that in the first place."

Her head tilted forward as she began to cry. Shaky sobs escaped her throat as I wrapped my arm around to hold her. For once, she didn't try to fight me.

Nine
Brooke

"What are you going to wear to the Winter Fair?" Sheila called from the living room while I worked on getting changed in my bedroom.

"I have no idea, why?" I answered as I shimmied out of my flour crusted work pants and sat down to put on sweats. It was a Friday night with a busy day ahead of me tomorrow so I was feeling relieved to stay in and do nothing. Today had kicked my butt with getting everything ready for the Winter Fair tomorrow. Even with Sheila and Autumn's help, it still felt like there was a lot left to get done. I grabbed a hair tie and threw my hair up into a wild mess of a bun and walked down the hallway to the living room.

I smiled when I saw that Sheila had already turned on the Christmas tree and started a fire while I was changing. This time of year was always hard for her because her custody agreement required that her ex-husband have the kids the week before Christmas, including Christmas Eve, and she got them again starting Christmas day. The loser didn't want them any other time of the year but had made sure to request the week before Christmas just to spite her, knowing that she loved doing Christmas stuff with them each night leading up to Christmas.

A lot of happy memories were made when they were little and thankfully he didn't ask for this ridiculous agreement until a few years ago, when they were old enough that he didn't have to do much to take care of them. Sheila had ten years of creating Christmas traditions with them before he robbed her of that. I grabbed the bottle of wine from the fridge and swiped two glasses from the wine rack before plopping down next to her on the couch. I pulled the cork out, relieved that it still had a satisfying popping sound when I opened it.

I filled two glasses and handed her one as I leaned back against the couch and pulled my feet up under me. We were due for another storm soon and the temperature was dropping quickly in anticipation of it. My toes felt like ice as I dug them down under the couch cushion.

"Did you finish your shopping for the kids yet?" I asked, hoping to change the subject from the Winter Fair.

"Almost," she sighed and took a sip of wine. "The older they get, the harder they are to shop for. I wish I could just buy them Legos and be done with it compared to what they actually want these days."

I laughed and lowered my glass to the coffee table knowing that she wasn't being dramatic when she said they were hard to shop for these days. I still needed to get their gifts and had no idea what to get them. It used to be that I could get them all similar gifts since they were so close in age and they would all share. But now that her oldest was sixteen and her youngest was twelve, those days were long gone.

"Well, Oliver thinks that he should get a car because he's sixteen and all of his friends have cars. I reminded him that he only has 2 friends and they drive the same car their daddy drove when I was in high school so it's nothing to brag about. Thomas wants everything Oliver wants so I had to explain that a fourteen-year-old was definitely not getting a car. We settled on a new video game. Megan wants to get her belly button pierced and Sally wants a boyfriend."

I laughed so hard as she ran down the list that I snorted, which got her laughing with me. She rolled her eyes and looked toward the fire, lost in thought.

"Sally is only twelve—she better not get a boyfriend before I do," I warned playfully, hoping to lighten the mood.

"Seriously, that's the same thing I told her. If mama can't date, neither can she." She winked and raised her wine glass to clink with mine that I had picked up from the table.

"Well, in all fairness, it's not that you *can't* date," I teased. "It's that you've been refusing to date since Rodney left."

Her face fell a little as sadness flashed across it.

"Sorry," I whispered. Her eyes looked up and met mine as she smiled.

"Don't be, it's okay. But I'll stay on this no-dating streak as long as I have to if that means she stops asking for a boyfriend. Maybe Santa can bring me a special friend this year, one that lasts a while and takes batteries." She giggled and lifted the glass to her lips before the blush could fully reach her cheeks.

"There's always Ryder's friend, he seemed pretty interested the other day when he couldn't take his eyes off you." I wiggled my eyebrows and waited for her reaction. As much as I had hated being there, I enjoyed watching as Sheila and Parker subtly checked each other out. It felt like being in middle school again when you were still terrified of someone finding out that you liked them. Okay, so maybe that wasn't limited to middle school.

"No way!" she shrieked as if I just proposed something ridiculous. She swatted her hand in the air as she finished her glass of wine and looked at me. "He was not looking at me, and there's no way that a guy like him would be interested in a girl like me."

"What's that supposed to mean?" I tilted my head slightly and gave her my full attention.

"It means that no one is looking to start something with a single mom of four rowdy kids and baby daddy drama."

"Sheila, you are beautiful, and caring, and one of the most giving people that I have ever met. ANY man would be lucky to have you, and I mean that. Rodney was a dumbass but he gave you four incredible blessings. Don't ever think any less of yourself because one person wasn't worthy of who you really are."

Her eyes filled with tears which forced mine to tear up as well. I grabbed the bottle of wine from the coffee table and refilled our glasses.

"So, are you going to let Megan pierce her belly button?" I asked, laughing at the expression she made in response.

"Over my dead body," she snorted.

"We had piercings at her age…" I smiled and shrugged my shoulders.

"Yeah, and I was pregnant a few years later, waddling down the aisle to collect my diploma before my water broke."

"Ah, those were the good days," I joked.

"Yeah, I miss those days sometimes. The late-night bonfires and drinking cheap wine while the guys ran around and acted a fool. We had some of the best nights together before everything fell apart."

I pressed my lips into a thin line, knowing where she was going with the conversation.

"Yeah, and some of the worst nights too."

"I saw you and Ryder talking on the bench after you walked out." Her tone changed, more sympathetic as I nodded in agreement.

"Then I saw him hold you as you cried."

I glanced up at her, the tears threatening to make a return if I started talking about it again.

"I've been wanting to ask you about it since then but I decided to be a grown-up and give you some space. More importantly, I was hoping that you would come to me, wanting to talk about it." She paused for a second and looked at me. "But, since that doesn't seem to be the case, I'm just going to keep pushing until you tell me what happened."

I blew out a deep breath and thought about what to say. The truth was that I had been wanting to talk to her about it since it happened but I could barely get my head around it myself.

"Ryder and I talked about the night that he left." I stared at the wall, watching as the embers of the fire danced wildly around the wood as it burned.

"And…"

"And he said that he knew he was stupid for leaving but he did it to protect me."

"Protect you? From what?" She pulled her brows together.

"From hurting me. He thought I deserved better than to fall for someone who was too afraid to admit that they had fallen in love with me. He said that he had been feeling it but when I confessed my feelings to him, it scared him and that's what forced him to leave with Lauren. Apparently, if I wouldn't have told him that I was falling in love with him, he never would have left with her."

I turned my attention back to her, chuckling when I saw her staring at me with her wine glass suspended in the air.

"What?!"

I nodded my head and let her have a few minutes to try to process it. Hell, it was days later and I was still trying to process it myself.

"That's so crazy!" she exhaled before taking a drink. "So, does he still have feelings for you?"

"I have no idea, but I doubt it. It's been ten years and a lot has changed since then. We've changed since then. I can't imagine that someone would just stay secretly in love with someone for that long and not move on."

"But you did," she said quietly, her words going straight to my heart.

64

Ten
Ryder

"You ready to do this?" Parker asked as he walked excitedly to the front door and turned the closed sign to open before unlocking the door. It was barely ten in the morning and I felt like I was on my eighth cup of coffee as my nerves shot through the roof in anticipation of the grand opening. With it being both four days until Christmas and also the Winter Fair, things around town were starting to feel busy, let alone trying to squeeze in the grand opening of a new sweet shop.

Ruby had been talking to everyone she could, letting them know about the grand opening and asking them to check it out before the Winter Fair started that afternoon. Parker and I had decided it was best to hype this up as a quick, three-hour event and then call it quits so we didn't have to compete with the fair. Besides, Ruby quickly reminded me that it had been awhile since I had been in town during the holidays and suggested that I plan to attend the fair to get back into the holiday spirit that I used to love when I was growing up. A lot of things in my life had changed since then but she was right. It was time for me to slow down and remember why I used to cherish this time of year.

I heard the bell chime above the door as I nodded yes, the anxiety quickly replaced by excitement. The door opened and I held my breath as people started floating in, spreading out and filling the room with the sound of holiday cheer as they started to browse. I had brought in a few extra tables and spaced them out with enough room to let people move freely through the shop, making the display counter and register the final stop on their path. Each table was covered with a beautiful deep red tablecloth and had a gold platter filled with samples as the centerpiece. Alongside each platter were small gift boxes filled with different chocolates that included a gift tag attached to the sheer, glittery wrapping paper Ruby had found at the last minute after I came up with the idea to offer gift sets last night.

Ruby and Parker had stayed up with me until two in the morning, packaging the chocolates as I made them. Ruby even had the brilliant idea to create kid-friendly boxes complete with chocolate-covered cherries decorated as mice. A few hours in and we were covered in chocolate when my mom came into the kitchen and found us, a huge smile on her face. Never in a million years would I have imagined that I would be laughing and joking with my mom in the kitchen that I grew up in, just like when I was little. She had a wonderful night and I woke up feeling hopeful that maybe she would have more good days now that I was back home. I shook my head to clear the thought as the first customer walked up to the counter with a handful of gift boxes in their arms and a smudge of chocolate in the corner of their mouth.

The first two and a half hours had flown by and I was busier than I could have ever imagined. It seemed that not only had all of the town locals come by but people from nearby towns came to check out the hottest new sweet shop in Stone Creek as well. The gift boxes had sold out completely within the first hour of us being open which was not something that I had expected. Before I could freak out about not having time to make more, Ruby came waltzing in with my mom, arms linked together with huge smiles on their faces. I was worried at first about having my mom out in public since no one knew about her recent dementia diagnosis. Seeing how happy she was with Ruby, I decided to embrace the holiday buzz around me, excited to see my mom out enjoying herself. The two of them quickly shuffled to the kitchen to help Parker as he tried to throw together more gift boxes with some of the chocolates we had for the display case.

It was almost time for the grand opening to be over, which I was thankful for because we had officially run out of chocolates aside from the few samples that were left on the empty tables. I leaned back against the counter and rolled my neck, trying to alleviate some of the tension that had been building all morning. I smiled and waved at Ruby as she and my mom left, the door chiming as it opened. I closed my eyes for a second, taking in the sound of pure silence. The sound of muffled whispers forced my eyes open to find Brooke and Sheila walking toward me, arms linked together as Sheila looked like she was trying to skip. Brooke shot her a quick look, causing Sheila's face to fall into a childish pout before she turned and smiled at me.

"Sorry we're so late, did we miss the big grand opening?" Sheila asked as she looked around. As her eyes wandered around the room I couldn't help but notice that she didn't seem to be looking for chocolate. I chuckled and shook my head as I leaned forward and rested my arms on the top of the display case.

"Parker is in the kitchen," I said with a wink as I nodded behind me. Her face was redder than the tablecloths covering the empty tables as she tucked her chin and looked down.

"Why would I care where he is?" Her voice was quiet as she mumbled the words, still refusing to make eye contact with me.

"I don't know, maybe because he hasn't stopped watching the front door all morning, waiting to see when you were going to come in." I glanced at Brooke and the loving smile on her face as she watched Sheila's head whip up with a beaming grin.

"Really?" she squealed excitedly before looking at Brooke as if she just found out that Santa was real. They exchanged a look that made me wonder what exactly they had been talking about when Sheila raised her eyebrows and subtly nodded in my direction. Now it was Brooke's turn to blush.

"Are you ready for the Winter Fair?" I asked Brooke, hoping to pull her attention to me. It had only been a few days since I had seen her but I was dying to talk to her after my confession. I had been so busy trying to get everything set up for the grand opening that I hadn't had a chance to go talk to her. I wanted to see how she was feeling after finding out that I was in love with her before I left for Nashville. I had played the conversation over and over again in my head the past few nights as I struggled to fall asleep, trying to dissect every tiny piece of it to see if there was any possible chance that she still felt the same way about me. Ten years might have passed but I still loved her as much today as I did the day I walked out and broke her heart.

"I think so," she sighed. "But it's too late at this point if not. Autumn is working on getting the last few things set up before we get over there, but we wanted to stop by and say congratulations on your grand opening." She smiled but it didn't fully reach her eyes.

"I'm sure you'll be just fine," I tried to assure her, not knowing what she was really worried about. The Winter Fair had always been a fun event, from what I remembered, and people were just excited to be out with each other, celebrating the holidays while they finished any last-minute holiday shopping.

"I wasn't planning for all of the extra traffic, but it seems a certain grand opening brought a swarm of people in from out of town so I'm worried that I won't have enough for the fair." She scrunched her face up in the cutest frown I had ever seen as she tucked a stray strand of hair behind her ear. I was thankful to see her wearing jeans and a cream-colored sweater instead of the loose clothes she wears in the kitchen. She looked like the kind of woman you would see in one of those cheesy Christmas movies, right before she finds the love of her life and they live happily ever after.

"Well, I'm about done here. I can help whip some stuff up for you if you want me to." I smiled and prayed that she would take me up on the offer so I could have a chance to spend some time with her today. Slowly, she looked around and raised an eyebrow at me as her gaze landed on the mistletoe Ruby had insisted on hanging at the end of the display case for decoration.

"I don't think you have anything left," she giggled, "Unless you're going to dip that mistletoe in chocolate, I think you're out of luck my friend."

I looked up and pretended to consider it, getting a laugh out of her in return. Her smile was finally a genuine one that lit up her face and had me smiling along with her. I felt her gaze land on mine as we shared this blissful moment before the kitchen door swung open and Parker walked out.

"You ready to get go—" he paused mid-sentence as his eyes landed on Sheila. I watched as she blushed and turned slightly to the side, pretending to look at the empty platter on the table beside her. "Hi, I didn't know anyone was here." He walked over and stood next to her as they quietly started their own conversation.

"So, back to what I was saying," I said gently as she turned around to look at me. "I'm happy to come over to your shop and help you if you think you might need more—what did you decide to make for this one?" I knew that every year Brooke created a new recipe for the Winter Fair and it was exclusive to that event. The people around town would anxiously wait for the fair, knowing that she wouldn't tell anyone what it was going to be before then. They would line up at her booth, making sure they grabbed a slice of whatever it was that she had decided to grace them with.

"You know I don't tell anyone what my secret item is before the fair," she warned playfully.

"Well, I'm not just anyone. I'm the king of chocolates that just sold over 300 gift boxes and cleared out an entire display case, as well as racked up over twenty custom orders before Christmas Eve. So yeah, I'm kind of special," I winked. "And if you tell me then I can help you and you can be the queen of the fair tonight."

"I'm the queen of the fair every year, nothing's going to change that." She smiled playfully and licked her lips. The action alone sent a chill through me as I imagined what it would be like to feel that tongue caress my body.

"Alright, *Queen*, but when you're panicking because you're running low and people are mad because they don't get some of whatever it is you decided to make- don't blame me," I smirked and shrugged my shoulders as I leaned against the counter behind me.

She glanced at Sheila before looking up at the clock hanging above me and sighed.

"Fine," she exhaled dramatically. "I'm making White Chocolate Cranberry Fudge. If you really want to help you can meet me in my kitchen in thirty minutes. I need to go make sure Autumn is ready to go, then I'll be back."

"I'll be there," I smiled and winked. She smiled and started to walk off before she paused and turned to look at me.

"Thank you, you really don't have to do this but I do appreciate the help."

I nodded and watched as she walked over to Sheila and wrapped her arm in hers as she whispered something in her ear. A few minutes later they waved and walked out the door.

"What was that all about?" Parker asked as he walked over and stood next to me, looking at the door.

"Making amends for the mistakes I've made along the way." I avoided looking at him as I started to think through my plan.

"So you're going to go spend your day making fudge as a way to say sorry for walking away and breaking her heart ten years ago?"

"No, I'm going to spend my day trying to make her see that I have never stopped loving her. I'll spend the rest of my *life* trying to make it up to her."

He smiled as he patted me on the back before walking back to the kitchen to clean up, leaving me alone with my thoughts.

Eleven
Brooke

I shifted my weight as I tried to balance the grocery bags on my hip and opened the door, letting it swing open and hit the wall as the bell chimed overhead. My fingers dug into the bottom of one of the bags, struggling to keep my grip on it as Ryder came up behind me, startling me.

"Need some help?" he asked as I jumped and let the bag go. His hand darted out and grabbed the bag before it could hit the ground. I blew out the breath I had been holding and looked up at him as he reached over and grabbed one of the other bags from me, lightening my load.

"You scared the shit out of me," I said as I walked inside and made my way to the kitchen, propping the door open with my hip as he followed behind me.

"You said thirty minutes," he answered with his brows pulled together.

"Huh?" I set the bags on the island that separated us in the middle of the kitchen and placed my palms down on the cool metal top as I looked at him, confused.

"You said to meet you in thirty minutes. It's been thirty minutes and here I am, meeting you." He shrugged his shoulders as if it should all make sense now. "I didn't mean to scare you, I thought you had heard me walking up behind you."

My heart was still racing as I tried to calm myself. Things were hectic when I went to check on Autumn. She had started early because a line of out-of-towners had already formed, anxious to see what *Sweet As Sugar* had in store for the fair this year. I did a quick inventory check while I was there and started to worry about how quickly we were going to run out of fudge before I ran over to the store for more supplies, knowing that I didn't have enough at the shop to make what we would need. What should have been thirty minutes felt like the longest hour of my life with everything being so rushed and stressful.

"I'm sorry, I'm just a little out of sorts right now," I tried to explain without getting into too many details. I forced a smile and turned my attention to gathering the things we would need so we could get started.

"Don't be sorry, I'm happy to help. Just tell me what you need me to do." He gave me the happiest smile that I had seen from him in I don't even know how long. When was the last time I had seen him happy? Like really, really happy? He cracked his knuckles and waited for my instructions.

"Okay," I sighed heavily and looked around for where to start so we weren't in each other's way. "Here are the bags of white chocolate," I said as I unloaded them from the bag and set them between us. "And here are the cans of sweetened condensed milk. I have the recipe written down on that paper by the measuring cups but once you have it all mixed you can just pop it into the microwave and we'll go from there."

He arched an eyebrow at me as he stepped back and folded his arms across his chest.

"You brought me over here to help you make *microwaved* fudge? That's a sin against all things sweet and you know it," he teased playfully.

I rolled my eyes and laughed.

"Trust me, I wanted to do something way better than *microwave fudge*," I said sarcastically, "but there wasn't enough time to try to pull something together with the extra work I've been doing with adding in a lunch menu around here. Trust me, I'm ashamed that I'm cheating too, but when you see it- it'll be beautiful. And what's even better is that it tastes *delicious,* so no one will even know." I smiled smugly and narrowed my eyes at him as he continued to raise his eyebrow at the situation.

"They will if I tell them…"

My eyes went wide as my hand flew to my hip, shaking my head as he watched with humor in his eyes.

"You wouldn't."

"Oh, I would…" He stepped forward and leaned against the island, bringing him close enough that I could smell the faint smell of his cologne. "But, I could be bribed… if the price is right."

"Oh so now you're blackmailing me?" I feigned shock as I grabbed a bag of chocolate chips and dumped them into the bowl before mixing in the can of milk and popping it into the microwave.

"You bet your sweet ass I am. I know what this secret is worth." He licked his lips as the grin spread further across his face.

"Okay, fine," I shrugged my shoulders. "What do you want?"

"Have dinner with me." There was a slight change in his voice as if it was hard for him to ask the question, his face hardening as he waited for my answer.

"Dinner?"

"Yeah, it's usually the meal that comes after lunch for those of us who stop long enough to actually eat," he said as he nodded behind me to the empty Snickers wrapper laying on the counter.

"Just dinner?" I asked cautiously, unsure of what he was asking. I heard the microwave ding, thankful for the distraction. I grabbed the bowl and pulled it out, setting it on the island as I stirred the chocolate and condensed milk together. I quickly added in the vanilla and dried cranberries, mixing thoroughly before I got too sidetracked.

"Did you have something else in mind that you were wanting to do in addition?" His face lit up with amusement as mine turned a dark shade of red. I stood, paralyzed, trying to force my mind to think of something intelligent to say back to him but it was completely blank. Taking full advantage of the situation and my stunned silence, he kept going. "Were you wanting to take me up on the offer to experiment with chocolate?" He slowly walked around the island, heading straight toward me as he slowly ran his fingers along the top of the island.

He stood in front of me, just inches away, studying me as my breathing started to get heavier. His eyes stayed fixed on mine as he reached over and slid the bowl over to him. Everything felt like it was happening in slow motion as he reached inside the bowl and ran his finger along the top of it, covering it in melted chocolate. He brought his finger to his mouth, his lips wet as they parted before he licked the chocolate off. I swallowed hard as I tried to look away, completely mesmerized by how seductive he made it look. Without thinking, I pulled my bottom lip in between my teeth as a soft moan escaped my throat. His eyes danced wildly as he watched my reaction, my chest rising and falling heavily.

I sucked in a deep breath and pulled my shoulders back, trying to force myself out of this fog.

"We better get moving before this sets, or *no one* will get any of my delicious *microwave fudge*," I said as steadily as I could. "And you better wash that finger before you touch anything else in my kitchen," I scolded as I shook my finger at him and turned my attention back to the fudge. I tried to look away before I saw the sexy, mischievous smile on his face as he chuckled and muttered *yes ma'am* before walking over to the sink and washing his hands.

Two hours later, the kitchen was packed with boxes of fudge that had already cooled and were packaged as well as the pans that covered the island from the last ten batches we had made. Never in my life had I ever made this much fudge. My feet hurt and my back was aching but I was relieved that we had plenty to get us through the rest of the fair, maybe a little bit extra left over. Ruby and Parker had come by earlier with Ryder's mom, Arlene, to help deliver some of the fudge that was ready to take to Autumn.

"Well, I think you are officially out of everything you need to make fudge. Are you good or do you need me to run to the store and get more?" Ryder asked as he leaned back against the counter and looked around the room.

"I think we're good, this should be plenty." I let out a heavy, tired sigh and rubbed the back of my neck with my hand, hoping to get some relief from the headache that was starting to build.

"Alright, well let me know what you want to do with the rest of these and I'll help you finish packing them up. Are some of these for samples or are you doing more gift boxes?"

"I would love to make as many gift boxes as possible. Lord knows that I need this to be a successful day," I muttered, not realizing what I had said until I felt his gaze on me.

"Why is that?" he asked as he started working on cutting the fudge into neat squares to be boxed up.

"Oh, it's nothing. I was just rambling on." I waved my hand dismissively, hoping he would drop the subject.

"I know you better than that, Brooke. Even after ten years, I still know when you're lying. So spill it, what's going on?" He looked up at me with a look of concern on his face. I rolled my shoulders and looked at him, frustrated that he still knew me so well.

"Mr. Rey, the guy who owns the strip mall, recently decided that he needed to raise the rent for those of us who still pay rent. Since three out of five of the shops own their space, he is only able to raise the rent for two of us and it's going to be a little steep. I'm trying to figure out how to bring in extra money to afford the increase that he's proposing. It won't go into effect until February but that's not that far away so I've been trying to save up what I can now. I don't want to be blindsided by it when he finally decides what he's doing."

"Mr. Rey? The old man that was tormenting people before I left? He's still around?" He frowned as he kept working on cutting the rest of the fudge.

"Yeah, he's still around. And still tormenting people."

"My dad never mentioned anything about him, I guess I just figured he died," he said with a fake scared face which made me laugh.

"That's probably because your dad didn't have to deal with him anymore. He bought his shop a few years ago after the original owner of the strip mall decided to sell it. Everyone had the option to buy their shops and those of us who didn't got stuck with Mr. Rey. I wanted to buy mine outright but

I didn't have the cash saved up for it." I smiled when I remembered sitting down and talking about my options with Ryder's dad before he passed. "You know, your dad offered to buy my shop for me. Offered me a loan that I could pay back over however long I needed. Anything to keep me from having to be indebted to Mr. Rey."

"Sounds like my dad," he smiled.

"Your dad was a good man, he really cared about this town and the people in it."

He nodded his head and looked away, sadness taking over the playful smile I had seen not that long ago.

"I'm sorry for bringing him up, I didn't mean to upset you," I said quietly as I worked on placing the cut fudge into the gift boxes.

"Don't be, it's nice to hear people talk about him. I just wish I would have come back sooner." He set the knife down on the counter and wiped his hands on the apron he was wearing. "And I'm sorry, I didn't know about the stuff with Mr. Rey. I feel like shit for opening a shop across from you when you're already busting your ass to find a way to stay afloat with the new rent increase. I should have looked into things more before I came barreling in and making a bigger mess of everything."

My shoulders slumped when I heard how remorseful he was. I never wanted him to feel bad about taking over his dad's shop. It wasn't like he was the reason I was working sixty hours a week and dreaming of burnt paninis when I actually got to sleep. I couldn't let him take the blame for the problems I had, they would have been there regardless of what he chose to do with the shop that his dad left him.

"Ryder, please don't feel bad. This has nothing to do with you. This is because I didn't buy the shop when I had the chance. It was a choice that I made, not anyone else."

"Yeah, but now we have competing businesses and I have a shop that is paid for. I don't have the same stress or worries that you do and that's pretty shitty."

"Your dad wanted to leave that shop for you. He was so proud of you and used to tell everyone about the incredible stuff you were doing in Nashville. He would have wanted you to take that shop and turn it into something that you were passionate about. And you did. Don't feel bad about that, feel good that you're doing what he would have wanted you to do."

He nodded his head as he closed the lid on the last box of fudge and slapped a sticker on it. He pushed it to the side and laid his palms flat on the island as he looked at me.

"Well, at least now I know why you had daggers coming out of your eyes the first time you saw me when they were hanging up the sign at my shop," he laughed.

I rolled my eyes and laughed with him.

"There were other reasons too, but that was literally the worst timing ever. I had just finished meeting with Mr. Rey a few minutes before I saw the sign going up. It felt like such a punch to the gut when I just learned that not only was my rent going up but now I had direct competition not even fifty feet away. It was a bad day, to say the least, and I'm sorry I wasn't more welcoming."

We stood there, lost in the moment for a few seconds before I heard the bell chime up front as the door opened. I wasn't expecting anyone and the confused look on his face as he shrugged told me that he wasn't either. I grabbed my phone off of the counter behind me and tucked it into my pocket as I made my way up front with Ryder right behind me. As I swung the door open and walked into the room, I froze in my tracks.

"Hey, Ryder, they told me I would find you here…" A wicked smile crossed her face as she looked from me to Ryder.

"Lauren?" he asked as shocked as I was to see her. Everything became a blur after that as the pounding in my ears grew louder, blocking out the bullshit words that came spewing out of her mouth.

Twelve
Ryder

"What are you doing here, Lauren?" I asked sternly as I watched Brooke stare at her in disbelief. Lauren smiled smugly at her but thankfully I don't think Brooke had noticed it. I wasn't sure if she even realized that we were still here, she looked that dazed and out of it. Suddenly, she snapped out of it and looked at me, ignoring Lauren.

"I need to get these over to Autumn, can you lock up for me when you're done?" she asked without waiting for my answer. A few seconds later, she was gone, loading up the last of the gift boxes in the kitchen. I worked my jaw back and forth as I stared at Lauren, waiting for her to tell me why the hell she was there. She hadn't changed any since the last time I saw her. Her hair was a little bit longer with fresh highlights that contrasted against the dark sandy brown color of her hair.

"I came to see you, to be with you, silly," she said as she reached over and ran a hand up my arm before I pulled away. Her brown eyes went wide as she flinched at my reaction.

"That's bullshit and you know it," I scoffed as I looked over my shoulder to see Brooke coming out with a box filled to the top with gift boxes. "Let me help you with that," I offered, turning my attention away from Lauren.

"I'm fine. Thank you," she snapped coldly as she pushed past me and walked out the door. I closed my eyes, hating that everything had been going so well between us today, only to be ruined by this.

"There wasn't a life insurance policy, Lauren. If you came for money, I don't have any. Why don't you go back to Nashville and look for a new soul to steal?"

She brought a freshly manicured hand to her chest and stared at me as a single, perfectly timed tear slid down her cheek.

"I can't believe that you would honestly think so little of me." She sniffled, pulling out all of the stops.

"Really? What else am I supposed to think? You cheated on me for years, told me how I would never amount to anything and then sent me emails with the details of your fuck fests with whatever his name was."

Her face fell as she lowered her eyes and wrapped her arms around herself.

"I'm sorry, I was a terrible person back then. I was immature and needed to grow up. I didn't realize what a good man I had until I lost you. But I know it now, and I want another chance." She reached out to touch my arm again. "Please."

"Look, I don't have time for this. And honestly, I'm not interested in starting anything up with you. That was a mistake in the past and I'm not looking to make it again. If you don't mind, I need to go so I can help Brooke." I nodded toward the door, hoping she would get my not so subtle hint.

"It's always been her, hasn't it?" She tilted her head to the side and waited as she crossed her arms over her chest.

"Yeah, it has. And it always will be. Now, I need to-"

Suddenly the door flew open as Ruby rushed in, looking frantic.

"She's gone, I can't find her anywhere!"

"Who's gone?" I asked as I rushed over to where she was.

"Your mom, she's gone. I took my eyes off of her for two seconds to talk to the pastor and she must have started to wander. I'm so sorry, Ryder, I'm so sorry." Her lip trembled as I pulled her in for a quick hug.

"It's okay, we'll find her. But we better get going before it gets dark."

She nodded her head yes as I gently walked her outside, Lauren right behind us. I patted my pocket to make sure I still had the keys to the shop that Brooke had dropped earlier when she was trying to get the door open with her arms full. Relieved when I found them, I pushed past Lauren, pulled the door shut and locked it.

"I can help you guys look for her, what does she look like?" Lauren said cheerfully with a smile.

"If you don't remember what this boy's mama looks like, you're not here for the right reason little girl," Ruby snorted as she started walking toward Main Street with my arm wrapped around her. I let out a laugh as I gently squeezed her and forgot all about Lauren as we started making our way through the crowd that was already filling the street for the fair. I tried to keep myself calm so I could focus as I desperately searched for my mom.

Thirteen
Brooke

"Thank you so much, have a Merry Christmas," I said with a smile as I handed the Crosbys the stack of gift boxes they had just purchased. They were one of the cutest couples in Stone Creek and married the longest. I watched as they stuffed the boxes into the tote bag that was hanging on the side of his walker and got situated before she wrapped her arm in his and they walked off together.

"They are just the cutest," Autumn said as she looked to where I was looking.

"Yeah, they are," I smiled, envious of the love they had. I had been desperately trying to forget about Ryder and Lauren from the second I left the shop, but it seemed every couple at the Winter Fair wanted to wait until I was back before they stopped by my booth. Love was all around me and I was fighting the urge to vomit.

I looked off to the side, watching as the crowd of people moved around each other, laughter and voices filling the air. This was my favorite time of the year and I absolutely loved the Winter Fair. It never felt like Christmas until the fair, then the next few days felt magical leading up to Christmas. I was lost in thought when I heard Autumn talking to a customer, her voice calm and soft like it was when she was speaking to someone older.

"I'm sorry, who are you looking for?" Autumn asked as she leaned forward to try to hear the woman better.

"Walter, I need to find my Walter."

"Your walker?" Autumn pulled her brows together and gave her a few minutes to try to get her thoughts together.

"No, my WALTER. Where is he? I need Walter!" The rising panic in her voice immediately grabbed my attention as I looked over and saw Ryder's mom. It had been a while since I had seen her. Hell, it had been a while since anyone in town had seen her. She looked the same as I had remembered, only now she looked panicked and out of sorts.

"Arlene?" I asked gently, loud enough for her to hear me over the buzz of the voices around us. She turned to look at me, not recognizing me as she stared blankly at me.

"Do you know where my Walter is?" Her eyes started rapidly scanning the crowd behind her as I made my way out of the booth and walked over to her.

"Hey, why don't you come sit down and I'll see if I can help you?" I gently reached out and helped her turn around, walking her into the booth and helping her sit down on the folding metal chair behind the table. I bent down and squatted in front of her so I could make sure that I was at eye level before talking to her.

"Arlene, do you remember me? My name is Brooke. I own the bakery across the street from Walter's flower shop." I wasn't sure what was going on but she seemed very confused and I was worried that she was having a panic attack, looking for her dead husband.

"Yes," she said slowly as she started to smile. Her hands reached for mine and I scooted a little closer so she could hold them. "I remember you, dear. My Walter always says such nice things about you. He really likes your banana bread." She giggled and her eyes lit up. I felt the tears well up inside as I thought back to the last time I had made the banana bread she was talking about. It was probably at least two or three years ago, around the time Walter started to act more stressed and everyone stopped seeing Arlene around town.

"That's right," I said cheerfully.

"Do you know where he is?" she asked sadly, gripping my hands a little tighter.

I felt a lump in my throat as I struggled with what to say. I needed to find Ryder and let him know that his mom was here but I also couldn't leave her right now. I had no idea what to do so I did the only thing I could think of, I lied.

"I don't know where he is but I'm going to ask my friend, Autumn, to go find him," I assured her as I slowly stood up and leaned in closer to Autumn. "Go find Ryder and tell him that his mom is at our booth and hurry," I whispered to her. She nodded and grabbed her phone, shoving it in her pocket before she took off jogging through the crowd.

I sat in the empty seat next to Arlene and tried to keep her calm while I waited for Ryder.

"Would you like some fudge?" I asked as I reached over and grabbed one of the gift boxes. "It's white chocolate cranberry." I smiled big as I held the box out to her, feeling elated when she took it. She reminded me of a little girl on Christmas the way she carefully undid the red ribbon that was wrapped around it before opening the lid and picking up a piece. Her eyes lit up as she held it in the air, the sugar sprinkles glistening in the lights that were strung throughout the booth.

"This looks too good to eat," she joked as she took a bite and closed her eyes. "But, I'm going to eat it anyway. My Walter is really going to love this."

I smiled and looked away, relieved when a couple from out of town came up and started asking questions about the fair. It felt like Autumn was gone forever but it was only twenty minutes before she came running back, breathless, with Ryder right behind her. Not too far off in the distance was Ruby. I watched as Ryder's eyes darted around, looking for his mother before the couple in front of the booth walked away and he spotted her handing me the money. He walked up to the booth and looked down at his mother who had a huge smile on her face.

"What's going on, mom?" he asked with a smile that matched hers.

"I'm selling fudge!"

"You are?" His eyebrows shot up high on his forehead as he turned to look at me. I shook my head and shrugged, letting him know that it was nothing.

"She's done a great job, I might have to hire her full time," I joked.

"I take my eyes off of you for a few seconds and you go find the prettiest girl at the fair with the best treats?" Ruby teased as she came around the back and gave me a quick hug before leaning down to hug Arlene.

"Did anyone find Walter?" Arlene asked, looking between all of us.

"Why don't we get you home and we'll talk about it on the way?" Ruby said softly, reaching down to help her up.

"Okay, I am getting tired." Arlene stood up and steadied herself against Ruby before turning to me. "Thank you for keeping me company, sometimes I get so lonely and I feel a little lost."

"It was my pleasure," I replied as steadily as I could. "Don't forget your fudge." I nodded toward the box, happy to see her smiling again as she picked it up.

"I can get her home if you want to stay at the fair," Ryder said to Ruby before she swatted his hand away as he tried to help Arlene walk.

"You go have fun, I'm tired too so I'll get her home and we'll talk later." She leaned in and planted a kiss on Ryder's cheek before turning to smile at me. "Have a good night, dear, and thank you for taking care of Arlene."

"It wasn't a problem at all, have a good night too, Ruby."

We stayed in awkward silence for a few minutes until Ruby and Arlene were out of sight and on their way to Ruby's car.

"Thank you for taking care of her, I'm sorry if she was any trouble." Ryder stepped to the side to let a customer get to the booth where Autumn was waiting. I walked around and followed him off to the side of the street to talk in private.

"It wasn't a big deal at all, I promise. She seemed really confused though, is she okay?" I didn't want to pry or stick my nose in his business but I was genuinely concerned about her.

"She has Alzheimer's and it's gotten worse since my dad passed. Ruby tries to help me as much as possible but my dad didn't want everyone in town to know about it. He was afraid that people would start talking about her and treating her differently so we all agreed to keep it a secret. That's why no one sees her around town anymore." He lowered his head and ran a hand along the back of his neck.

"I'm so sorry, that has to be really tough. Has she had it for a long time?"

"A couple of years. My dad was handling it on his own and then when he passed, I knew that I needed to come down here so I could help out. I wasn't planning to come back but then everything happened so quickly and I feel like I haven't been able to catch my breath since."

His eyes met mine and I could see the pain and grief behind them. I felt terrible for the way I had treated him when he first got back, especially now that I knew everything he had been dealing with on his own that no one knew about. He selflessly gave up the life he had created for himself in Nashville to come back and take care of his mom. My heart tightened at the thought of how much he'd been through and how much he was still going through after seeing Arlene tonight. I wondered if he had to remind her daily that her husband had died?

"If there is ever anything that I can do to help, please let me know." I tilted my head to the side, hoping he would look at me and feel the emotion I felt for his situation.

"Thank you, I appreciate it."

Suddenly I saw Ryder's expression change as his face hardened and goosebumps tickled my skin. I didn't have to turn around to know who was behind me.

"Hey, I heard they found your mom. Looks like we can pick up where we left off," Lauren said as she grabbed his hand and started to pull him away. I chewed the inside of my cheek as I looked away.

"Yeah, I better get going," I said, giving a tight smile to both of them as I turned to walk away.

"Brooke…" he called as I kept walking without looking back.

Fourteen
Ryder

Sunday used to be my favorite day of the week because it was the only day that I took off and tried to get the stuff done that I needed to throughout the week. But today— today was by far my least favorite day—ever. I had spent the night awake, restless, trying to figure out how to get Brooke to talk to me so I could make things right but every time I tried, Lauren got in the way.

I had tried to talk to her a few times at the fair before everything closed down. I even tried to help her pack up and take everything back to her shop before I was quickly dismissed. I tried calling her, thanks to Sheila who had taken pity on me and given me her number, but she refused my calls. And my voicemails. Even my text messages. I was two steps away from walking over to her house and banging on her door until she let me in before Parker talked me out of it and told me what a crazed lunatic I would look like.

So instead, I'd spent my night pacing around the kitchen until I came up with the brilliant plan to bake her an "I'm sorry" loaf of banana bread. Okay, so technically I made fifteen, but there was an entire bunch of bananas that were about to go bad and needed to be used. Around four this morning, I finally sat down in my dad's recliner and closed my eyes, hoping that there would be some sort of magic in the old thing and he would tell me what to do.

Two hours later, I was woken up by the sound of a frying pan clattering around in the kitchen when I found my mom attempting to fry some eggs for breakfast. I rushed in and pulled her away from the stove before she could burn herself and offered her a slice of banana bread to hold her over while I cooked breakfast. I felt bad that we were suddenly out of eggs—oops, but she seemed to forget all about them when she smelled the bacon cooking.

I yawned as I slid the bacon onto her plate and grabbed the toast that had just popped up in the toaster. I walked into the living room and smiled when I saw her curled up under a blanket in my dad's chair, watching tv. She looked so calm and relaxed that it started to make me feel the same way. I set our plates down on the coffee table and sat down on the couch beside her, thankful for a peaceful moment with her.

"Breakfast is ready, mom," I said, pulling her attention away from the tv.

"Thank you, son," she smiled warmly and reached over to

pat my hand. It took me a minute before I realized that for the first time since I had been back, she knew who I was. She wasn't confused, thinking that I was my dad.

"You know who I am?" I asked gently, turning to look at her. Her eyes were a dark green this morning and looked full of life.

"Yes, dear, I know who you are. Your dad told me that you were coming home soon, I've been expecting you." Her voice was cheerful and my heart sank when I realized that she wasn't as clear-headed as I had hoped.

"Dad's not here anymore, mom." I tried to force a smile on my face for her sake, but my body refused to do it.

"I know dear, he told me that too."

"What do you mean that he told you? When did you talk to dad?" I asked against my better judgment as I studied her.

"In my dream last night. Your dad comes to talk to me often or at least it feels like he does. I don't know how many times exactly. But he talks to me and keeps me company until he's ready to come back for me." She let out a heavy sigh before she turned to look at me. I tried to look away, to blink away the tears before she saw them but I was too late. She reached over and ran her thumb across my cheek, wiping the lone tear that had managed to escape.

"It's okay, dear, you don't have to be sad." She smiled and pulled her hand away as she turned back to watch the tv and I knew that my moment with her was over. I had lost her again.

We ate breakfast in silence as she watched her show and laughed at the slapstick comedy. I tried to loosen up and enjoy it but my mind was too busy focusing on everything else that I needed to get done. Ruby would be here soon to spend time with my mom so I could get to the shop to work on the custom orders that I needed to get going ASAP. It was three days until Christmas which left me exactly two days to get everything ready by noon on Christmas Eve. I was feeling the pressure as I checked on my mom one last time before going to the kitchen to clean up the mess. A few minutes later, I heard the front door open as Ruby walked in and smiled at me.

"Morning, sunshine. You look like shit," she joked as she pulled her coat off and hung it on the hook by the door before pulling her scarf around her neck and hanging it up as well. "How was your night or should I not ask?"

"I didn't get more than a few hours of sleep and that was after I was up until four baking over a dozen loaves of banana bread. I woke up to mom trying to cook herself breakfast."

"Oh, Lord. Was she okay?" Ruby's face fell as concern filled her eyes.

"Yeah, I got to her just in time. She had turned on all four burners without realizing she had turned on any of them. She was seconds away from catching the sleeve of her robe on fire when I walked in."

Ruby blew out a breath and folded her arms across her chest.

"We're going to have to do something else, it's getting worse with trying to keep her safe. You can't be here to watch her 24/7," Ruby said sympathetically.

"I know, I know," I sighed. I had been thinking the same thing all morning but still had yet to come up with a way to fix it.

"I'm not trying to overstep, you know that, but I could come live here with her if you want?"

"Ruby, I couldn't ask you to do that." I shook my head knowing that she would be giving up so much to do that for us.

"Why not?" She pulled her brows together and narrowed her eyes at me.

"Because you love that house, you've lived there as long as I've been alive. You have your own life and if you move in here with us, that life will be drastically changed." I explained as I worked on loading the dirty dishes into the dishwasher.

"Ryder, I loved that house when Johnny was still alive and our kids still came to visit. Now I'm there all by myself in that big house and I'll be honest with you—it gets a little lonely there sometimes. It's not full of the warmth and happiness that it used to have. That all disappeared a long time ago and that's okay. I still have memories of the happy times but I don't need a massive, empty house to keep me happy. I would rather be close to the people who still make me happy. And I need to feel *useful*," she said dramatically as her eyes almost popped out of her head.

I stopped for a minute and thought about what she was offering. While it would be great to have her here with me all the time to help with my mom, I still felt bad for taking advantage of her generosity.

"I feel like I would be taking advantage of you," I said cautiously.

"Oh hush," she waved her hand at me and shushed me. "I wouldn't offer to do it if I didn't want to. Besides, my youngest daughter is moving back with her husband and three kids— they could use the space without me in their hair all the time. But I don't want to be in yours either, so you'll need to be honest with me on whether you think this could even work."

"I would love to have you here, and I know my mom would love the company as well," I said with a warm smile and held my arms out for a hug. She wrapped her arms around me and for a moment it felt like a huge weight had been lifted.

"I will try to stay out of the way," she whispered before she pulled away.

"You could never be in the way, Ruby. Thank you for coming to help us, it means a lot to me."

She reached up and patted my cheek, the way she always did ever since I was a little boy.

"Well, I hate to rush off but I've got a ton on my to-do list today," I apologized as I glanced back at the sink full of dishes that didn't fit in the dishwasher.

"Don't worry about any of that, I'll take care of it later. Go, get your stuff done and don't forget to stop by and make amends with Brooke." She winked playfully.

"It's not that easy, but thanks." I forced another smile, feeling that heavy weight quickly returning.

"Sure it is. You love her. She loves you. Now you just fix whatever needs fixing and then you two can make up and be together," she said happily as she walked over to the sink and gently pushed me out of the way so she could get to the dishes.

"I don't think love is involved here, in fact, I'm pretty sure she's back to hating me," I winced as I said it and waited for her to ask what I had done this time.

She studied my face for a few seconds before turning her attention back to the sink full of dishes as she pushed them out of the way to slide the stopper in before turning the hot water on to fill the sink.

"There are a lot of things that I know nothing about in this life—technology, new slang, the inability of the youth in this town to wear pants that cover their ass—but one thing that I do know is true love when I see it. And Ryder, I've seen it between you and Brooke. Now it's up to you to show her how much you've loved her all along."

"We were starting to talk, and she even agreed to go on a date with me."

Ruby arched an eyebrow in surprise as a smug smile pulled across her face.

"Okay, so maybe she wasn't fully on board with it being a date, but either way—she agreed to have dinner with me. But then Lauren showed up and every time Brooke sees her, she just shuts down and walks away. I don't know how to get her to see that there's nothing between Lauren and me. It's like the worst decision of my life from ten years ago is this constant thorn in my side, intent on fucking up every chance I get with Brooke."

"Once you deal with the thorn, the pain will go away and the true beauty of the rose will shine through," Ruby replied softly.

I ran a hand down my face and shook my head before looking at her. It was way too early in the morning to be solving riddles.

"Okay, I have no idea what that's supposed to mean so I'm going to leave you with your Beauty and The Beast riddle while I get going or I'm never going to get anything done today." I leaned forward and planted a kiss on her cheek as she chuckled before I left.

Thirty minutes later, I was standing outside Brooke's door, freezing my ass off as the snow fell around me, holding a loaf of banana bread wrapped in saran wrap with a red bow on top. I waited a solid thirty seconds before I reached forward and rang the bell again, knowing she was inside as I had just heard her talking to someone a few seconds ago. I could hear her voice drift further away and wondered if she knew it was me at the door and was purposely not answering it.

I was about to ring it again when the door swung open and Sheila smiled at me from the other side. Her hair was pulled up into a knot on her head, looking like she had just woken up. Which she probably had given that she was still wearing red and green striped Elf looking pajamas. I bit down on the inside of my cheek to keep from laughing as I took in the sight.

"Good morning," I said as I tried to push the laughter out of my voice. I pressed my lips together in an attempt to keep from smiling and giving it away that I thought she looked ridiculous.

"Morning," she said, eyeing me carefully.

"Is Brooke here?" I asked as a gust of wind blew right past me, sending a cold chill through me.

"Maybe… depends on what you want." She raised an eyebrow as she made no attempts to move from the doorway. I arched my brow back at her and tilted my head to the side.

"Fine," she sighed as she grabbed the side of the door and pulled it back, making room for me to go inside. "You can come in but you better share whatever that is that you brought with you." She pointed toward the loaf of bread before walking past me and sitting down on the couch as Brooke walked into the living room and stopped in her tracks when she saw me. I burst out in laughter when I saw that she was wearing matching elf pajamas and looked as ridiculous as Sheila. I turned my head and pretended to cough, hoping that it would look believable. As I turned back around, I found her glaring at me, hands on her hips.

"I'm sorry, I wasn't expecting you two to match," I explained as I pointed a finger between the two of them. "I brought you a loaf of banana bread." I held it out for her even though she made no attempt to move any closer to grab it.

Sheila looked nervously between the two of us before getting up and grabbing it from me before returning to her spot on the couch.

"Thanks," she said cheerfully as Brooke and I remained in our silent stare down.

"Look, I wanted to talk to you about what happened last night," I said, taking a step toward her. She held up her hand and stopped me.

"Don't bother, it's fine. I've heard everything that I needed to hear."

I felt like my heart sank and formed a knot in my stomach.

"I don't have any idea what you've heard but I would really like it if you would at least let me tell you my side of the story."

"Look, whatever you thought this was going to be between us—it's not. I'm sorry, I'm glad that you're back as a friend but I don't mess around with guys who are engaged." Brooke's tone was so harsh and full of anger that I almost missed what she said.

I pulled my head back in confusion and turned to look at Sheila, hoping she would be able to help me shed some light on what had just happened. *Engaged??* What the actual fuck was going on?

"I'm sorry—what?" I asked as I turned my attention back to Brooke and took a step closer to her. She quickly took a step back, acting like she was afraid to be that close to me. Not that I blamed her, I usually treated people who were engaged like they had the plague too but for different reasons. Before Brooke, that was something that I had hoped I would never catch—feelings.

"Lauren told us last night about the big news," Sheila said quietly from the couch. "She showed us the ring and told us about how you guys had just gotten engaged before your dad died and that you had to come back right away to get things situated while she wrapped things up in Nashville. But now she's back for good since you guys are getting married here in the spring."

Her eyes locked onto mine and I saw the desperate plea of her asking me to tell her that it was all a huge lie, one big misunderstanding. The problem was- it wasn't.

Fifteen
Brooke

"You did the right thing," Sheila assured me as she covered
her slice of banana bread in butter before leaning back
against the couch to eat it. Ryder had left twenty minutes
ago and I was still fuming from seeing him. After Lauren
cornered Sheila and me in the parking lot last night and told
us all about her engagement, I hadn't stopped being livid.
Livid with Ryder. With myself. With the entire situation.
At first, we brushed Lauren off as telling another lie for
attention but when she held her hand out and showed us
the vintage wedding ring that had once belonged to Ryder's
grandma, we knew that she wasn't lying.

"I don't even know what the right thing is anymore," I
mumbled as I shoved the last bite of bread into my mouth,
not bothering to wipe away the crumbs that had fallen
onto my shirt. I glanced down at the elf pajamas I was still

wearing and shook my head, embarrassed that Ryder had seen me in them.

"At least this bread is really good, I was *starving,*" Sheila said as sat forward and grabbed the knife to cut another piece. More than half the loaf was already gone as we ate as if we hadn't had a meal in days.

"I'm surprised it's not covered in chocolate," I snorted, feeling petty but not having anything else to complain about.

"I bet it would be delicious covered in chocolate," she teased while wiggling her eyebrows suggestively. I rolled my eyes and pushed the plate away from me as I leaned back on the couch and pulled my legs up underneath me.

"You want everything covered in chocolate." I reached across and poked her leg with my toes.

"What can I say? I LOVE chocolate." She let out a dreamy sigh and batted her eyes at me.

"Well, I guess you missed your chance to have Ryder cover you in chocolate now that he's engaged."

"Oh please, he never wanted to cover anyone in chocolate but you. And from the look of how he was acting this morning, I think he still wants to."

"Sheila, he's ENGAGED. Like past the point of just seeing someone—he's about to marry someone and spend the rest of his life with them. I think that offer is long gone. And it should be, I don't mess around with a guy in a relationship." I shrugged my shoulders and tried to sound as tough as I wanted to feel.

"I just don't get why he would be flirting so much with you and then ask you to dinner, if he was engaged? That doesn't make any sense," Sheila said as she turned to face me on the couch.

"Well, maybe he's just that kind of guy? He knew that Lauren was cheating on him before he left—maybe it doesn't bother him. Maybe he's just a terrible guy and we never knew it."

Sheila was quiet for a few minutes before she spoke, thinking through what she wanted to say.

"Do you really believe that?"

"What?" I asked.

"That he's a terrible guy who would cheat on his fiancé with a woman he's been in love with all of his life?"

I swallowed hard to push away the emotion that was threatening to bubble up inside. It didn't matter what I thought. It was too late. He was with someone else and the past no longer mattered.

"No, I don't think he's a terrible guy," I said sadly. "I think he's a wonderful guy who stepped up to help a friend in need yesterday and who has gone out of his way to apologize for something he did ten years ago. But I also think that this wonderful, loving guy—he doesn't belong to me. He never has and he never will."

I pulled my hand up into my sleeve and used it to wipe away the tears that ran down my face, a harsh reminder of what my reality actually was.

<u>Sixteen</u>
Ryder

I was working on my eighth batch of chocolate truffles when I heard a knock on the door. I set down the silicone mold I had just finished washing and dried my hands on the towel that hung by the sink before going up front to see who was showing up on a Sunday. I was supposed to be closed. As I got closer to the door, it looked like whoever had been there was already gone. I unlocked the door and opened it, checking to see if there was possibly a package left outside since my car was in the parking lot. It would be odd but not unheard of in a small town. After all, everyone knew where you were at all times, whether you wanted them to or not.

As soon as I opened the door, I saw someone pop around from the side of the wall, scaring the shit out of me. My hand flew to my chest as I took a step back and glared at Lauren. She giggled and stepped closer, the smell of her perfume floating around her. I narrowed my eyes and glared at her before stepping to the side to block her from coming in. Her smile was quickly replaced with a pouty frown as she pursed her lips and looked up at me under the thick coat of mascara she was wearing.

"What are you doing here?" I snapped angrily.

"We need to talk," she said sweetly as she reached forward to touch my arm. I jerked back and she flinched the same way she did every time she's tried it since she's been back.

"The only thing we need to talk about is why you're still wearing the ring you were supposed to send back with Parker and why the fuck you've been going around town telling everyone that we're engaged and you're moving back to be with me."

Her brown eyes darkened, turning almost black, as she looked at me with anger etched on her face.

"Did you really think that you could end our engagement through a text message? Do you think that's how you break up with a girl like me?" she shrieked, forcing the vein in her forehead to protrude.

"You know as well as I do that we were never really engaged. The whole thing was a stupid, drunken mistake that I've regretted since the moment it happened. Why don't you just give me the ring back and you can be on your way, looking for the next soul to steal from some poor, unsuspecting chump?"

"I'm not here to return the ring," she said through gritted teeth. "I'm here to talk about our future and to make plans for it."

"Lauren, we don't have a future together and you know it. Like I've already told you, there wasn't a life insurance policy—I didn't inherit any butt loads of money. I'm as broke now as I was when you walked out and left me in Nashville."

She turned her head to the side and looked out at the parking lot as she worked her jaw back and forth in frustration. Her foot started to tap anxiously on the sidewalk while she tried to figure out a new angle.

"The ring, Lauren…" I said impatiently as I held out my hand. "Now!"

The stern tone in my voice startled her as she jumped and turned to face me, fear in her eyes. I blew out a heavy breath and raised my eyebrows at her as I stared her down, getting tired and frustrated with her games. I pushed my hand toward her and nodded down at it, her eyes following mine. She shook her head and rolled her eyes as she pulled the ring off of her finger and tossed it into my hand. My hand quickly closed around it before it bounced off and fell to the floor.

"Happy?" she sneered as she smirked at me.

"Tremendously," I taunted as I gave her the fake smile that I knew she hated. "Now, why don't you do us all a favor and go back to Nashville where you belong?"

"You just made the biggest mistake of your life, you know that?"

"No, I made that mistake ten years ago when I walked away from Brooke and fell for your bullshit and followed you to Nashville."

She licked her lips and I expected her to say something, instead, she turned on her heel and walked away. I watched as she stormed off, the sound of her boots fading in the distance. I slid the ring into my pocket and went back inside to finish the custom orders that felt like they would never end.

Not even ten minutes later, I was in the middle of another order of truffles when I heard a knock on the front door again. I grunted and walked up front, expecting to see Lauren back for more. Once again, there was no one at the door when I got there, making me even more irritated than I was before. I was about to turn around and go back to the kitchen when I heard another soft knock. I whipped the door open, having had enough of Lauren's bullshit.

"What the fuck do you want now?" I bit out before looking to see who was there.

Brooke's face dropped in surprise as she stared at me in disbelief.

"I'm sorry, apparently this isn't a good time," she said quickly as she turned to walk away. "Sorry for bothering you."

"Brooke," I called out as I leaned against the open door and smiled when she stopped and turned around, shoving her hands into her coat pocket as the snow blew around her. "Do you want to come inside and get out of the cold?"

She smiled tightly and nodded before rushing over and shivering as she slid in between me and the door. There was already a light dusting of snow in her hair which started to melt once she was inside where it was warm.

"I don't want to bother you if you're busy. You seemed mad," she said as I closed the door behind her and locked it.

"I thought you were Lauren," I explained with a heavy sigh. She nodded and looked away as if the topic of Lauren made her uncomfortable.

"I am not Lauren." She chewed her bottom lip nervously before glancing out the window to avoid looking at me.

"No, you certainly are not," I assured her, feeling more relaxed now that she was here. "So, what's up?" I asked as I started walking back to the kitchen and nodded for her to follow me. I realized then that I had been in her kitchen but she hadn't been in mine yet. It was a weird thing to feel proud about but I knew that if anyone would appreciate all of the work it took to convert the flower shop into a functional kitchen, it would be Brooke.

Her eyes were wide as she looked around in amazement, her fingers lightly running across the stainless steel surface of the counters as she walked around and took everything in.

"This is an incredible kitchen," she said cheerfully as she glanced over her shoulder to smile at me. "You would never know how big it is from the outside but now that I'm in here, I can't imagine going back to my small, rickety kitchen again," she teased.

"Well, you're welcome in here anytime but I have to warn you that I may put you to work if you're in here," I winked and walked over to the island to work on the truffles. Her smile spread across her face as she looked around and saw the stuff I was working on. She pushed her lips together to try to hold the laughter in and ended up snorting instead. I laughed as she turned around to try to hide her face while the blush crept up her fair skin.

"What's so funny?" I asked as I leaned forward and rested my palms on the island.

"Nothing," she snorted, bursting into another fit of laughter. "I'm sorry, really, it's not that funny," she insisted as she tried to be serious. I arched an eyebrow and waited.

"Fine," she laughed. "I was just wondering if there's anything that you don't cover in chocolate? But then I remembered that the bread wasn't dipped in chocolate this morning, so there ya go—I have my answer." Her eyes danced wildly with amusement as she watched my reaction.

"Trust me, I know my way around chocolate and I wouldn't be so quick to judge my skills if I were you." I winked as I pulled my lower lip in through my teeth and watched her squirm.

We stayed quiet, staring at each other for what felt like minutes. I was scared to look away and lose this moment with her. Suddenly she shifted her weight as her fingers started pulling at a loose thread in the sleeve of her coat and I knew that she was back to feeling anxious and nervous around me again.

"I just wanted to come by to say that I was sorry for how I reacted this morning and to thank you for the bread. Who you're dating—or rather, engaged to, isn't any of my business and it wasn't fair for me to treat you that way. It's not like we were dating." She shrugged and tilted her head to the side as if she was trying to remember if there was more that she wanted to say.

"You're welcome for the bread and you did have a right to react the way you did. I've made it very clear that I'm interested in you and recently admitted to having feelings for you before I left. Then, I asked you to have dinner with me and I spent the day helping you make fudge. I would hope that those things would show you how much you really mean to me, Brooke. And I'm sorry that you found out about the engagement before I could tell you, I really am." I ran a hand through my hair and prayed that she would be open to listening, given that she had that scared look on her face that usually meant she was about to run away. I needed her to listen to me and hear my side of what happened.

"I just don't get why you would go through all of that effort with me if you were engaged to Lauren?" She narrowed her eyes at me.

"It's a long story but I promise, I wasn't engaged to her. She just didn't want to believe it."

"I'm going to need more than that," she said with a laugh.

"Right after my dad died, I was sitting at home one night, holding this ring in my hand that was given to me after his funeral. My aunt told me that my dad wanted me to have the ring so I could find a woman who deserved me and spend my life with someone who made me happy. I had a couple of beers and the next thing I knew, I was buzzed. Lauren had been calling since I got back but I hadn't bothered to call her. Out of nowhere, she shows up, trying to be my 'friend'. Apparently, in my drunken stupor, I asked her to marry me and move back to Stone Creek with me," I sighed.

"I don't remember proposing to her, obviously, but the next day I woke up next to her in my bed and she was wearing the ring. She insisted that I was so romantic when I proposed to her and got furious when I told her that I didn't remember it. It's been a nightmare ever since."

"Do you think that you really proposed to her while you were drunk? That maybe it brought up feelings that you still had for her?"

"No, I honestly don't. I think Lauren found the ring and took advantage of the situation. She was way too anxious to help me with settling my dad's estate so I think she's just stayed around because she expects that there was a life insurance policy or some sort of inheritance that I haven't told her about."

"Well, that sounds like Lauren," she muttered and looked away.

"Yeah, it really does."

"I ran into her on my way over here today." She looked up and watched as anger flashed across my face. I hated that Lauren always had to be vengeful and knew that she was the one who had approached Brooke, again.

"Technically, I was on my way to my shop but she felt the need to stop me and tell me that you were all mine and that I could finally have her sloppy seconds because she was through with you. I wasn't planning to come over to see you but when she kept watching me with those hateful eyes, I came over just to spite her." She laughed and shook her head. "It's stupid and petty, I know."

"Well, then I guess I owe her a thank you," I said with a crooked smile.

"Why's that?"

"Because thanks to her, it got you over here so we could talk. I was starting to run out of ideas on how to get you to let down that damn wall you keep putting up every time I come around."

"I don't put up a wall…"

"Yes, you do, and it's ice-cold and frozen." I stepped around the side of the island and walked toward her.

"Are you insinuating that I'm ice cold?"

"Mmmhmm," I whispered as I stood in front of her, lowering my head to look at her. "But don't worry, I know exactly how to heat things up and thaw that frozen heart of yours."

"Does it involve chocolate?" she asked as she rubbed her lips together. I shook my head and smiled, pretending to be insulted as I gently reached out and put my hands on her hips. I felt her body immediately tense before she slowly exhaled and looked up at me.

"It sure does," I licked my lips suggestively. "Nice, warm, chocolate."

She giggled as I lowered my head and placed my lips on hers, feeling relieved when I felt her hand wrap around my head as she kissed me back.

Seventeen
Brooke

"I'm coming," I called as I pushed the gold hoop earring through my ear and stopped to glance at myself in the mirror as butterflies fluttered around in my stomach. I ran a hand down the front of my dress, feeling nervous about wearing it out in public. Sheila had convinced me to purchase it months ago, and then it sat in my closet the entire summer because I was too scared to wear it. The dress was a vibrant fuchsia color and hit right above my knee. It was fun and flowy, hugging my curves perfectly without being too tight or provocative. It was a whopping two degrees outside and the snow was steadily falling, but I wanted to look sexy for my first official date with Ryder.

It was Christmas Eve which meant that everything would be closing down early and we wouldn't have any dinner options unless we wanted to drive to another town. I had no idea what he had up his sleeve. He just said to get dressed up and be ready by seven. I pulled on the white faux fur coat that Sheila had loaned me for the date and grabbed my purse from the counter as I swung the door open and smiled. Ryder brought a hand to his mouth as he took a step back and looked me up and down, making me both anxious and horny at the same time. When was the last time that a guy had ever looked at me like that?

His cologne drifted in with the light gust of wind that blew past him, making me feel weak in the knees. He looked incredibly sexy in his dark denim jeans and navy cashmere sweater, a different look than I had seen him in before.

"You look incredible," he said softly as he stepped inside and gave me a quick kiss on the cheek.

"Thank you," I said with a smile, feeling giddy and excited to be with him.

"Are you ready to go?" He stepped to the side and held his hand out for me to walk in front of him. I glanced down at the snow that was sticking to the ground and started to reconsider whether I should go change into something that didn't involve a six-inch heel that would definitely break in the snow.

"Maybe I should change my shoes real quick, I don't want to risk falling or freezing my butt off in these," I said warily as I looked back at him.

"We're not going far, I think you'll be okay," he assured me with a smile as we walked outside and I locked the door behind us.

A few minutes later and we were pulling into the parking lot of the strip mall. I felt a bubble of disappointment when I realized where we were.

"Don't look so sad, you have no idea what I have planned for you," he joked as he put the car in park and hopped out before running to the other side to help me out. He held my elbow as he led me over to the door of his shop and quickly worked to unlock the door. A few seconds later, we walked inside and I waited while he went over to turn the lights on. It took a few seconds for the lights to come on but when they did I found a beautiful table in the middle of the room, set up for us.

It was a round table with a white tablecloth and a slim vase with a single red rose in the center. The table was set beautifully with matching china and a bucket filled with ice off to the side with champagne inside. Everything was perfect and reminded me of being in one of those fancy 5-star restaurants that I always see on tv. I looked over my shoulder and smiled at him, still in shock over how much effort he had put into this.

"I know everyone closes early tonight, so I thought I could make you dinner instead," he whispered in my ear as he came and stood behind me, wrapping his arms around my waist as I leaned against his tight chest.

"It's beautiful, thank you. But you didn't have to go through all of this trouble for me." I looked up at him and gave him a light kiss on the lips.

"That kiss alone was worth it," he teased before walking me over to the table and pulling out a chair for me to sit. "Have a seat and I'll be back in a few minutes. And while I'm gone, here's some champagne to get this evening started." He winked and pulled the cork out, the popping sound sending a thrill of excitement through me. Slowly, he poured some into each of the glasses on the table, handing me one before he rushed off to the kitchen.

I lifted the glass to my lips and took a sip, closing my eyes as the cold bubbles made their way down my throat. A few minutes later, he returned with two bowls of salad and a basket of fresh bread. Everything was perfect and I felt like royalty the way he was pampering me. After we finished our salad and bread, we sat together for a few minutes enjoying our champagne before the timer in the kitchen dinged to let him know that dinner was ready.

The kitchen door swung open as he carried our plates in, the robust aroma floating through the air as it made my stomach growl. He set my plate down in front of me, a thick piece of steak cooked just the way I liked it with a side of roasted potatoes and steamed asparagus. My mouth watered as I waited for him to get situated before diving in.

The room was quiet and peaceful as we ate, the soft sound of Christmas music playing overhead. I worked through eating as much as I could without making myself sick and finally had to throw in the towel. Literally. His eyes lit up when he looked over and saw my plate, nearly empty, as I leaned back and wished I had worn something a little looser than this dress.

"Did you enjoy dinner?" he asked as he raised his glass to his lips and took a drink.

"Very much, thank you," I replied softly. "Though it does make me regret wearing this dress. You know, it wasn't this tight when I left." I laughed and playfully pulled at the fabric of it.

"You can always take it off," he winked and leaned back in his chair.

"As tempting as that sounds, I'm not that kind of girl." I pursed my lips and narrowed my eyes.

"Just trying to be helpful." He laughed and held his hands up in defense.

"I'm sure you are," I laughed. "Besides, it wouldn't be fair that I was the only one who was naked…"

"If that's the problem, I have the solution," he said as he stood up and started to pull his sweater over his head. He stopped midway, showing me his ripped abs before pulling it back down and laughing. My heart was racing at the thought of him taking it off.

"Tease," I joked and took another sip of champagne. His eyebrows shot up and he tilted his head to look at me.

"Did you just call me a tease?"

"Yup."

"Oh baby, you have no idea just how much of a tease I can be," he said cockily as he slowly grabbed the bottom of his sweater and pulled it up and over his head. In one swift movement, he tossed it across the room and stalked toward me. I swallowed hard as I watched him, his eyes fixated on me as he got closer. He grabbed my hand and placed it on his stomach, slowly moving it down to the top of his jeans.

"You want more?" he asked, his voice suddenly gruff. His hand held mine firmly in place as I felt his breathing increase the longer I touched him. I crossed my legs and scooted closer to him, wanting to feel the heat that was coming from his body. I stared at him, his perfectly chiseled body, and thought about running my tongue across it.

"Do you want more, Brooke?" he asked again, this time there was new desperation in his voice. I nodded my head unable to speak. He sucked a deep breath in and pulled away, rushing off to the kitchen. I sat there stunned, trying to figure out what just happened when I saw him come back with a bottle of chocolate syrup. He handed it to me and nodded for me to take it.

"You're kidding, right?" I asked in disbelief. I had always heard of people using food items in foreplay but he wasn't actually serious about covering each other in chocolate. Was he?

"Not even a little. You wanted to know if there was anything that I don't cover in chocolate- here's your answer." He stood before me the same way he was a few seconds ago as I held the cold bottle of syrup in my hands. I looked up at him, uncertain of whether he was serious when he gave me the sexiest smile I had ever seen.

Slowly, I stood up and with a shaky hand, pulling open the top of the bottle before gently squirting it onto his chest. He sucked in a deep breath as the cold chocolate touched his skin and let it out steadily as he waited for me. I leaned closer and lowered my head, looking up at him from under my eyelashes as I trailed my tongue along the chocolate that was running down his chest. I felt his body react beneath my touch, spurring me to keep going. I lazily ran my tongue across his body, closing my eyes as I imagined things going further.

I moved my head lower, sliding my tongue along his stomach until I reached the top of his jeans. I dropped to my knees and looked up at him as I unbuttoned his jeans before slowly sliding the zipper down, letting them fall to his ankles. His eyes stayed watching me while I slid my hands up his thighs and pulled down his boxer briefs, freeing the massive erection that greeted me. I kept my eyes on him as I reached for the bottle of chocolate syrup and squirted it onto his dick. His eyes closed immediately as he took in a deep breath, his fists clenched by my head.

I leaned forward and licked the syrup, spreading it along the length of his cock before pulling back and taking him in my mouth. I heard him gasp as I took him in further, pushing as deep into my throat as possible. It was making me wet to feel how his body was responding to me as I pulled back and began to work his shaft with my hand while I sucked on his head. He was big, to say the least, and at one point, I had to use both hands to fully wrap around him while I sucked him harder. His breathing quickened as his hand reached out and grabbed a fistful of my hair, turning me on even more.

"Fuck, Brooke, I'm gonna come baby," he moaned breathlessly as I grabbed onto him even tighter and quickened my pace as his body trembled in front of me, hot liquid shooting down the back of my throat.

Once I knew that he was done, I slowly pulled him out of my mouth and stood up. He was gorgeous in his jeans and fitted sweater, but he was downright sexy standing in front of me completely naked.

"That was fucking incredible," he mumbled as I leaned up to kiss him on the cheek. He turned my head toward him with his finger and kissed me deeply, wrapping his arms around me as he reached down and grabbed my ass.

"Now it's my turn to make you feel incredible," he said as he grabbed my ass and lifted me up, my legs wrapping around his waist as the sheer fabric of my panties felt the warmth of his dick. His fingers gently spread my ass cheeks apart, forcing the thin piece of my thong to ride up. He walked over and sat me down on one of the longer tables by the window and stepped back. I quickly reached down to fix my dress when his hand reached over and stopped me as he shook his head no. I glanced behind me, the cold chill from the glass window reminding me that we were at the very front of the shop and that if anyone were walking by, they would be able to see us.

"What if someone sees us?" I asked as I nodded to the window behind me.

"They can watch me fuck you as an early Christmas present," he answered as he moved closer, still fully naked as his dick started to get hard again. My eyes went wide at the thought of someone watching.

"Does that bother you? Knowing that someone might be watching as I eat you out?" He stood in front of me and gently moved my hair to the side as he reached behind me to unzip my dress. He pulled the zipper down slowly as he kept talking quietly in my ear. "What if they stop and watch as I finger you? Maybe it's a guy who finds it so fucking hot that he whips his dick out and jacks off while he watches us. Do you want that? Do you want some other guy to come while he watches me fuck you, Brooke?"

I was panting, my chest heaving, my body desperate for him to touch me.

"Yes," I moaned as he slid the fabric of the dress down my body, letting it pool at my waist. He stepped back and looked at me while I squirmed anxiously.

"Take off your bra," he instructed as he reached down and grabbed his cock. I felt the air rush out of me as I watched, the site of it exhilarating.

I reached back and unhooked my bra, letting it fall as his eyes stayed glued to me while his hand worked himself faster.

"Lay down on the table and take your dress off."

I nodded and slowly did as he asked, making sure to keep my balance so I didn't fall. The table was long and felt sturdy enough, but I didn't want to risk anything. I was about to reach down and take my heels off when he stopped me.

"Leave them on," he whispered. "Same with your panties."

I smiled nervously and laid down, feeling on display as he walked over and bent down in front of me. He reached down and pushed my panties to the side as he kissed my pussy, catching me off guard. My head whipped up as I looked down at him. I wasn't against oral sex, not by any means, but I definitely wasn't expecting him to just dive on in. I gave him a puzzled look before he looked up above us and laughed.

"Mistletoe," he nodded at it. "It doesn't specify where I get to kiss you so I figured I would just take advantage and go for what I wanted."

"I'm surprised it's not covered in chocolate," I teased as I laid back down.

"No, but you're about to be," he murmured as he rushed over and grabbed the bottle from the table where I had left it. Within seconds I felt the cold rush as it drizzled across my body before the warmth of his tongue started to lick it up. My body was on fire as his tongue worked it's magic on me, forcing me over the edge as I screamed his name while riding my orgasm on the cold surface of the table beneath me.

I was feeling on top of the world when he made his way back up, looking completely satisfied himself with chocolate smeared on his chin and cheeks. He helped me up and I thought we were going to move somewhere else to finish. Instead, he pushed the tables apart and had me stand behind one of them as he gently spread my legs apart while I was still wearing my heels. He leaned forward and kissed the back of my neck as he plowed into me, taking me from behind in front of the window.

"I bet his dick is so hard right now, watching me fuck your tight little pussy. I bet he wishes he was in here with us. He could stand in front of you while you suck his huge cock, taking him down your throat while my dick fucks you from behind. Do you want that, Brooke?" he groaned as he pounded me even harder. Suddenly, I imagined the picture he was describing and felt like I was going to come again.

"Yes, Ryder, yes! I want that so bad," I screamed as I reached down and pinched my nipple with one hand, bracing myself against the table with the other while he fucked me with my panties still on. A few seconds later I was climaxing a second time while he came inside of me.

Eighteen
Ryder

Last night had been absolutely amazing with Brooke and I was still grinning about it this morning when I sat down with my mom and Ruby to open presents. The night had been exactly what I had hoped it would be- easy going and romantic, but then it took a turn and ended up being hotter than hell.

In all of my wildest fantasies, I never would have pictured Brooke being such a sexual person but I loved that about her. The way her beautiful face looked as she held me in her mouth, sucking me dry. Or the way her body responded to my touch, coming undone with the dirty words I whispered in her ear as I plowed into her. I would have bet money that she was a sweet, gentle lover but after last night I was itching to see what else she liked.

After we finished opening gifts, I wandered into the kitchen to fix a late breakfast, biding my time while I knew Brooke was at her parents' house for Christmas. She mentioned that she planned to be home around lunchtime so we could get together before her dinner plans. I was anxious to see her and felt down that I couldn't spend the entire day with her, but we had also both agreed that we would wait a little longer before we started telling anyone that we were dating.

"So I heard you had your own little Christmas party last night," Ruby said slyly as she buttered her toast before looking up at me.

"Hmm?" I pretended not to know what she was talking about as I shoved a fork full of scrambled eggs into my mouth and chewed.

"Really? Okay," she laughed and held her hands up. "I won't pry but I will say that a little birdie told me they saw you with a pretty girl going into your shop last night, and both of you looked dressed to the nines. Maybe like you were on a date?"

She wiggled her eyebrows and laughed, causing me to laugh as I tried to avoid the knowing look she was giving me.

"Okay," I said as I set my fork down on the plate and pushed it away. I wiped my mouth with a napkin then turned my attention to Ruby. "I took Brooke there last night as our first official date, and I made her dinner. That's all there is to it. Just a friendly, first date." I shrugged and leaned back against the couch and raised my cup to take a sip of coffee.

"From what I heard— it was more than just "friendly" from what you did in front of the window."

I spit coffee across the room, feeling the burn as it came out of my nose. I reached for the napkin and started to dry my

face as Ruby burst into laughter next to me.
"Oh man, I was just waiting to see if I could get a rise out of you but I didn't think you'd really fall for it!" She laughed louder as she slapped her knee. My mom turned her attention from her show on tv and smiled as she watched us, not having any idea what had just happened.

I finished cleaning up the mess, too embarrassed to look at Ruby knowing that she would know there was truth to what she had said about the window. I kept my head down and cleaned the coffee table so it was cleaner than the day my dad bought it. I tossed the used napkin on my plate and got up, clearing the other plates as I shook my head and laughed.

It was finally time to go see Brooke so I said goodbye as quickly as I could and snuck out of the house before anyone could ask where I was going. As if she was just as excited to see me as I was to see her, Brooke was waiting at the door as soon as I pulled up. I grabbed her gift from the passenger seat before I got out and jogged up the few steps to her door, my spirits dropping when I saw the look on her face.

"Hey, Merry Christmas," I said as I wrapped her in a hug. I was relieved when she hugged me tightly, knowing that I wasn't the problem. "What's wrong?" I asked as I pulled back and looked at her. I could tell she had been crying, her makeup slightly smudged under her eyes. She shook her head and we walked inside as she closed the door behind us.

"Brooke, what happened? Why are you so upset? Did something happen at your parent's house?"

"No, no, nothing like that," she sighed and sat on the couch as

I followed and sat next to her. She reached over and picked up an envelope off of the coffee table, handing it to me. "That was under my door when I got back from my parents."

I opened the envelope and pulled out a letter from the scumbag landlord at the strip mall. The letter had been typed up and a sloppy signature from him attached to the bottom. I quickly scanned it again, not believing what I was reading. In bold letters in the middle of the page was the confirmation that he was raising her rent by almost $500 a month, effective February 1st.

"You've got to be kidding me," I mumbled as I ran a hand down my face. "This guy has some nerve."

"You're telling me." She leaned forward and folded her hands together in her lap. "I have no idea what I'm going to do. Obviously, there's no way I'm going to be able to come up with an extra $500 in rent by February, and my only other option is to back out of the lease agreement and find another place. But that would also mean that I would have to spend money that I don't have and build something from the ground up." She looked at me and took a deep breath before leaning back and cuddling one of the throw pillows in between us.

My mind was racing, going back and forth between thoughts of how to cheer her up and how to smash someone's head in without getting caught. Suddenly, I had the perfect idea and prayed that she would jump on board.

"Move in with me," I blurted out, getting a panicked look from her in return.

"Not like- move into my house- move in, but move into my shop with me. We can combine our businesses and have a one-stop-shop where people can get a variety of sweet treats."

"You're crazy, I couldn't do that." She shook her head and eyed me as if I might be on drugs.

"Why not? There's plenty of room for both of us, you've been in the kitchen and loved it. We make similar stuff so it's not like we'll have clashing aromas. It's perfect." I smiled, hoping she would consider it.

"I don't know..."

"What else are you going to do? You said it yourself that your only other option is to back out of the lease and find something else. This can be that something else."

"Are you sure you want to be around me all the time? Can we even work together without getting in each other's way? And what would I do about Autumn?" Her questions came out in one long-winded breath that had a hint of excitement.

"We seemed to do just fine the other day when we worked on the fudge together. There's also the other half of the kitchen that's empty— I can get another counter and an extra fridge so we both have our own designated space. And I don't have anyone up front so Autumn can come on board too."

"Okay, this might actually work. What is the monthly rent?" she asked as her eyes lit up.

"Zero."

"No Ryder, I want to pay my share. Please give me a number and as long as it's lower than the one on that paper you have a deal."

"I'm not going to charge you, Brooke."

"Why not?"

"Because you don't worry about stuff like that with someone you love," I said quietly.

"Someone you love?" She raised her eyebrows as hope flashed across her face. I nodded yes and looked deep into her eyes.

"Brooke Hansen, I knew I loved you in sixth grade when you were the only girl who didn't freak out when we had to dissect the frog in science class. You shed one single tear and said your goodbye before you jumped on in. I love that you go after what you want in life, and I hope that will always be me. I love you."

"I love you too, Ryder," she whispered as she leaned over and wrapped her arms around my neck to kiss me. As she pulled away, I instantly missed the way her lips felt on mine.

"I made you something for Christmas," she said happily as she reached over and grabbed a neatly wrapped box and handed it to me. I smiled and reached for hers that I had set on the table.

"Okay, but open mine first," I insisted as I handed it to her. She smiled as she took it and slid the ribbon off before her grin spread across her face as she opened it and pulled out a piece of chocolate-covered mistletoe.

"I know how much you've been looking forward to the chocolate covered mistletoe," I teased as I reached over and grabbed it, slowly moving it over her body like a metal detector. "But the real gift is that you get to pick where the mistletoe lands and where you want me to kiss first."

I watched as her cheeks flushed before her hand lowered the mistletoe exactly where I wanted it. I quietly mumbled *ho ho ho* in her ear before giving her the gift she *really* wanted.

Four hours later, she was scrambling to slide her shoes on as we rushed out the door to head over to Sheila's house for dinner. We were already late but after her last orgasm, neither of us was able to move as quickly as we needed to.

"Does she know I'm coming with you?" I asked as I glanced over at Brooke sitting next to me in the passenger seat.

"I didn't have a chance to tell her but it's Sheila and she loves surprises. She'll be thrilled you're there."

I felt guilty for showing up unexpectedly but once Sheila opened the door and saw me, her face lit up brighter than her giant Christmas tree in the corner as she wrapped her arms around me and pulled me in for a hug.

"I'm so happy you are joining us!" She exclaimed as we walked in and hung our coats on the rack by the door.

"Thank you for having me, I'm sorry about the last-minute surprise," I said apologetically.

"Don't worry about it, the more the merrier," she brushed me off and walked past us into the kitchen where she grabbed two glasses of wine and turned to hand them to us. "Besides, it's nice to have company this time of year," she smiled and looked past us at Parker who was sitting at the table playing a game of Uno with her kids. I wrapped my arm around Brooke's waist and pulled her close to me as I felt my heart overflowing with happiness.

<u>Epilogue</u>
Brooke

"Hey buddy, you're in my work space," I giggled, Ryder's hands sliding around my waist as I tried to frost the cake I was working on.

"I can't help myself, that cake looks good enough to eat but you look even better," he teased, his voice low in my ear as he planted kisses down my neck.

"Your face is cold." I shivered as a chill ran through me.

"Yeah, it started snowing again as I was leaving the store. It's supposed to come down pretty heavy the rest of the day. I'm hoping we can still make it to our reservation but if not, I'll make you a nice dinner here like I did for Christmas Eve…" His hand slid up my waist and cupped my breast, forcing me to drop the spatula in my hand before I ruined the cake. I leaned against him and enjoyed feeling his hands roam over my body.

"Christmas Eve was great, but I think New Year's Eve was even better," I said as I tilted my head up and kissed his chin, the scruff of his beard tickling my lips.

"Mmmm," he murmured against my ear as he pressed himself against me from behind. "Who knew that champagne would still be so bubbly when you licked it off someone's stomach?" he teased as he stepped back and let go of me. We both knew that if we didn't stop now, we would be naked and going at it, and this cake wouldn't be ready by two-thirty when Mrs. Forsythe came in to pick it up. I turned to look at him, smiling when I saw him pull off the black beanie that I had knitted him for Christmas. It was a last-minute gift idea and I was so nervous that he would hate it. He's proudly worn it almost every day, except for when I bug him to wash it every now and then.

I went back to working on the cake, smoothing out the sides before adding a few decorative flowers to the top of it. Once everything was finished, I added the cake topper and stepped back to look at my work. I heard the bell ding up front, knowing that Mrs. Forsythe was here for the cake. I carefully slid it into the box and closed the lid. It felt good to be working at a slower pace than I was before the holidays and for once, I wasn't slammed with orders while adding on the stress of creating a larger menu that I honestly couldn't keep up with if I tried.

I walked up front and got a big hug from Mrs. Forsythe before she rushed off with the cake for the baby shower she was hosting in a few hours. The day was quiet for the most part, though we did have a rush this morning with a few stragglers coming in to get chocolates *after* they had realized it was

Valentine's Day and hadn't thought to get anything ahead of time. Everyone else had placed custom orders with Ryder for his chocolate-covered strawberries or chocolate truffles. We had spent the past few days working for hours on the custom orders, all of which had been picked up this morning.

I pushed myself up on the counter behind the register and wrapped my legs around Ryder's waist as he stood in front of me. Slowly I leaned forward and kissed him, feeling all of the stress and tension melt away as his hands stretched across my thighs. He reached forward and grabbed my ass, pulling me closer to him as we deepened the kiss. Out of nowhere, the door opened and the bell chimed as we pulled apart and looked to see who had come in.

"Ugh, you guys really need to get a room. No one needs to see that," Sheila whined as she walked over and sat down at one of the tables across from where we were. She pulled her gloves off and tossed them on the table in front of her. "Especially not those of us who are alone and sad on Valentine's Day."

I jumped down off the counter and walked over to sit by her, squeezing her shoulders gently as I passed by. I pulled the chair out and sat down, offering her the goofiest smile I could come up with. She rolled her eyes and looked away, trying to pretend that she didn't think it was funny. I crossed my eyes and pushed the tip of my nose up as I started snorting, making myself look absolutely ridiculous. Suddenly she burst into laughter, leaning back in her chair as she started to relax.

"There, now that's better," I said as I leaned back and smiled. "Where are the kids today?"

"Oliver is out shopping for his girlfriend and took Megan along with him so she could help. Thomas and Sally are with their dad, trying to help him find the perfect ring so he can propose to his new girlfriend."

"No!" I gasped and covered my mouth. "He's going to *marry* her? They barely know each other…" I knew that they had started to get serious at Christmas but surely they weren't ready to get married six weeks later. My heart ached for Sheila knowing that even though she didn't want to be with Rodney, it still wasn't easy for her to hear about him getting married either. Suddenly I felt my anxiety start to build when I thought about whether to share our news with her today or wait a while. Like a long, long while.

"He says that it's true love and the kids seem to love her, so I guess it is what it is." She shrugged, the sad puppy look returning to her face.

"I'm sorry, honey. I know that this isn't easy for you." I reached over and squeezed her hand. "Do you want something sweet to cheer you up?"

"I figured you guys would be sold out, with everyone being in love and all," she sighed. "Does Ryder have any chocolate covered strawberries left, or are those gone with my hopes and dreams?" She glanced over at him as he stood behind the register and listened.

"Don't worry, girl. I got you," he winked and walked back to the kitchen. I had no idea what he was up to since I knew damn well that there weren't any strawberries left after we used the last of them this morning for a last-minute order.

"How are things going between you guys?" Sheila asked once he was gone.

"It's going good," I sighed and thought about how much to get into with her, and how long before Ryder came back.

"Oh come on, I might be lonely and depressed but that doesn't mean that I don't want all the juicy gossip." She lightly smacked my arm and laughed. I rolled my eyes and shook my head, glancing at the kitchen door to make sure he was still back there.

"Things are good. Ruby has been really helpful with taking care of his mom which has taken a lot of the stress off of him that he was feeling when he first came back. We've been spending so much time together that we kind of decided to live together…" I swallowed hard and looked up at her as I waited for her reaction.

"Oh. My. Gosh!" she squealed excitedly. "Brooke—that's amazing! I'm so happy for you guys!"

"Thanks," I said, relieved that she wasn't upset about it. I knew that Sheila was a sensitive person and I didn't want to add any additional upsetting news to what she had already been given today. "He's been staying at my house and we found that it works better for everyone. Ruby is handling everything there and we still go by and visit a few times a week to check in on his mom. But overall, everyone seems to be adjusting to the changes easily."

"Maybe because it's just meant to be for you guys to be together. And then you guys can get engaged and start having babies, and live happily ever after."

"I think you're a few steps ahead of us," I joked. Ryder and I had talked a lot about our future recently and both agreed that marriage and kids could wait a while. We weren't in a hurry to rush into anything. For now, we just wanted to enjoy our time with each other.

"Well, all in due time. But at least you guys are doing good working together AND living together. That has to say something about your relationship."

"I am honestly so surprised by how easy it's been working together. We don't get in each other's way and that kitchen is so big that we can do our own thing and not worry about what the other is doing. It's been wonderful. And, I'm really grateful that I don't have to worry about Mr. Rey anymore. Or busting my ass to come up with the extra $500 a month that he wanted. I'm kind of sad that they're already putting something else in over there but it was time to move on."

"Have you guys come up with a name for this one? Or is it just going to be 'the sweet shop' like everyone around town has been calling it?"

"Ugh," I groaned. "That's the one thing that we can't agree on. Neither of us can think of a name that fits both sides. He does a lot of fancy chocolates and I bake a lot of cakes and pastries. There just doesn't seem to be a name that fits both. Or at least not one that we both like."

"Alright, *The Sweet Shop* it is," she laughed.

I laughed with her, straining to listen as I heard Ryder's voice in the kitchen. Once I realized that he was probably on the phone and not talking to me, I stopped listening and shifted my attention back to Sheila.

"So, have you heard from Parker?" I asked cautiously, hoping that I wasn't bringing up another sore subject.

"No," she sighed heavily and sunk lower in her chair. "Last I heard, he made it back to Nashville but I haven't heard much from him since then. It's my own stupid fault for liking someone who doesn't even live here."

"Maybe you should try to call him? I know things ended awkwardly for you guys but maybe he's feeling too scared to reach out to you?"

"Awkward is an understatement. We had a one night stand on New Year's Eve after we decided that when the ball dropped, so should our pants. It was fun, and it was definitely good—but maybe next time I shouldn't jump the first drunk guy I see."

"I think you're being a little hard on yourself. It's not like you didn't know him and he was some stranger. You guys spent almost every day together from Christmas to New Year's and were texting nonstop when you weren't together. He was just as interested in you as you were him."

"Maybe…" She took a deep breath and slowly let it out. "But it still feels weird. He left shortly after that and we've barely talked since then, other than him letting me know he got there okay. It felt more like he was one of my kids checking in, than a possible boyfriend."

I pulled my lips into a thin line, feeling bad for her that she was having to go through this. I had asked Ryder several times if he knew what was going on with Parker but either he was lying to me or he really hadn't heard from him either.

"I'm sorry honey, I really am. I know how much you liked him."

She nodded as we heard the door to the kitchen swing open and Ryder walked out, carrying a plate of chocolate-covered strawberries. I arched a brow as I looked up at him, wondering where they came from. He held the plate out for Sheila, waiting for her to take one, as he winked playfully at me. Next, he extended the plate to me for me to take one of the last two strawberries. I picked one up and watched as he sat down on the other side and lifted the last strawberry from the plate.

"Happy Valentine's Day, ladies," he said as he lifted his chocolate-covered strawberry in the air to cheers us. "I hope that you feel loved every day of the year and that you feel cherished today."

Sheila took a bite of her strawberry after tapping it against Ryder's, a look of disappointment sitting heavy on her face as she chewed it.

"Don't look so sad, Sheila," Ryder said playfully. My eyes almost bulged out of my head as I kicked him under the table, trying to pull his attention away from her so he didn't make things worse. When he looked at me, I raised both eyebrows and gave him a pointed look.

"What?" he shrugged innocently as he shrugged his shoulders. "Can't I be the optimistic one who thinks her day might just turn around?"

I gave him a puzzled look as I watched the smug smile spread across his face. A few seconds later we heard the door open and the bell chimed. My eyes spotted him first, staring in disbelief at what I was seeing as he walked in and headed for our table.

"Excuse me, miss, I was wondering if you had plans tonight?" His voice was low as he stood behind Sheila, a smile spread across his face as he held a beautiful bouquet of red roses in one hand and a box of chocolates in the other. Slowly, she turned around, her face lighting up as she saw him. She dropped the rest of her strawberry to the table and jumped up, her hands covering her mouth as she stared at him.

"Is that a yes?" he asked playfully before reaching out to offer her the roses. Her hands trembled as she took them, the smile still plastered on her face.

"Yes, Parker, that's a yes," she said happily and wrapped her arms around his neck as she kissed him.

"See," Ryder said, leaning across the table to talk to me. "Sometimes everyone gets a chance to be happy."

I smiled and leaned over to kiss him, knowing that he was right. For once, everyone was happy and things felt like they were going in the right direction.

Chocolate Covered Mistletoe Desserts

I want to thank my wonderful readers who sent me some of their favorite holiday dessert recipes, some of which were used in the book. As a special treat, I'm including a few of them here for everyone to enjoy!

**Please note that I am not the person who created these recipes nor am I taking credit for them. Recipes were received from multiple readers who wanted to share their favorite desserts with others. Any likeness to other recipes found in general search results is purely coincidental.*

White Chocolate Cranberry Fudge

Ingredients:
6 oz dried sweetened cranberries
2 - 12 oz bags of white chocolate chips
1 tsp vanilla extract
14 oz can sweetened condensed milk
Pinch of salt
Sparkling sugar sprinkles (optional)

Directions:
1. Line an 8x8 pan with parchment paper, making sure to cover the sides of the pan.

2. Combine white chocolate chips and sweetened condensed milk in a large microwave safe bowl and cook for one minute, then stir to combine. Continue stirring so the ingredients can melt together, however it may need an additional 30 seconds in the microwave. Continue to stir until it's completely melted together.

3. Once melted, combine the salt, vanilla extract, and dried cranberries. Mix thoroughly before using a spatula to pour into an 8x8 baking pan. After the fudge has been poured into the pan, you can add the sparking sugar sprinkles, making sure to press them into the top of the fudge.

4. Set fudge in the fridge for a few hours to allow it to set up completely before cutting. Be sure to store the fudge in an air tight container, either at room temperature or in the refrigerator.

Peppermint Chocolate Dipped Oreo Balls

Ingredients:

16 ounces of white chocolate (melting wafers or chocolate chips)
1 Package of Oreo cookies
8 oz cream cheese
½ tsp peppermint extract
48 crushed peppermint candies

Directions:

1. Use a food processor to mix the Oreos and cream cheese together until well combined. If you don't have a food processor, you can use a rolling pin to crush the Oreos inside of a Ziplock bag, then combine with the cream cheese. Make sure both are mixed thoroughly.

2. Using a spoon or an ice cream scooper, scoop out small balls of the mixture and roll into 48 balls. Place the balls on a parchment paper lined cookie sheet and freeze for thirty minutes, or until hard.

3. While the balls are freezing, use a rolling pin to crush the peppermint candies into smaller pieces. Spread them out on a piece of parchment paper and set to the side for later.

4. Once the balls are firm, take them from the freezer and set them to the side while melting the chocolate for dipping.

5. In a large, microwave safe bowl, combine the white chocolate and peppermint extract. Start out with melting in 30 second increments, stirring between each one, until fully melted.

6. Using a fork, dip each ball into the chocolate, then roll it in the crushed peppermint candies. Once fully coated, transfer them to a clean piece of parchment paper to allow them to harden.

Be sure to store peppermint chocolate dipped Oreo balls in the fridge (for food safety)

Candied Pecans

Ingredients:

2 cups pecans
4 Tbsp salted butter
3 Tbsp brown sugar
1 Tbsp white sugar
1 tsp cinnamon
Pinch of Salt

Directions:

1. Melt butter on medium-high heat.

2. Add in the pecans, making sure to coat each one while constantly stirring.

3. Next, add in the brown sugar, white sugar, cinnamon and salt. Stir constantly until the sugar is completely melted.

4. Spread on parchment paper to cool.

Chocolate Truffles

Ingredients:

2- 4 oz Semi-sweet chocolate bars

2/3 cup Heavy cream

1/2 tsp Vanilla extract

Toppings: unsweetened cocoa powder, crushed nuts, or sprinkles.

Directions:

1. Chop the chocolate into small pieces and set aside in a heat safe bowl.

2. Place the cream in a sauce pan over medium heat and cook for 2-3 minutes or until cream is simmering.

3. Pour the cream over the chopped chocolate and allow the mixture to rest for 3-5 minutes, allowing the cream to melt the chocolate.

4. Add in the vanilla extract and slowly stir until the chocolate has completely melted. Cover the top tightly with a piece of plastic wrap to avoid condensation. Refrigerate for one hour, or until firm.

5. Scoop the mixture into 1 tablespoon-sized mounds, then roll each one into a ball shape. If the chocolate gets too soft and starts to melt, you can chill it until it becomes easier to work with again.

6. Roll each ball into the desired toppings then place them on a parchment paper lined cookie sheet. Return them to the fridge to chill until firm.

7. Store your truffles in an airtight container in the refrigerator. Be sure to take them out at least fifteen minutes before serving to allow them to be enjoyed at room temperature.

Decadent Irish Cream Fudge

Ingredients:

2 cups milk chocolate or semisweet chocolate chips
1/2 cup sweetened condensed milk
1/4 cup Bailey's or other Irish Cream Liqueur
1 teaspoon vanilla extract

Directions:

1. Line a pan with parchment paper and set aside.

2. Add the chocolate chips and sweetened condensed milk to a microwave safe bowl and heat for 30 seconds. Stir with a spoon to make sure the chocolate is mixing with the sweetened condensed milk, microwaving for another 30 seconds if needed. Be careful not to overheat and burn the chocolate.

3. Once the mixture is melted, add in the Bailey's and vanilla extract.

4. Use a spatula to pour the fudge into the pan, smoothing out the top after scraping the sides of the bowl clean.

5. Let set in the refrigerator for a few hours until firm before cutting it.

Acknowledgements

Just as this book is short and sweet, so are my acknowledgements!

A huge, heartfelt thank you to all of the readers, bloggers, and Instagrammers who quickly jumped on board to read this one and told everyone about it. You're the best!

To my alpha readers— Chelsea and Azucena- you ladies already know how much I love and adore you! I'm so thankful for both of you and couldn't imagine writing without you helping me along the way.

I want to say a huge thank you to my beta readers for giving me quick feedback and helping me to get this wrapped up before it's due date, thank you!

I also want to thank Tillie and Richard for working your editing magic on yet another book! You guys are the best!

Thank you to my family and friends for your constant support, I appreciate each and every one of you.

About the Author

Samantha lives in the southwest with her husband and two small children after abandoning her childhood dream of living in a cabin in Colorado when she found that she couldn't afford to live there and was deathly allergic to the woods. When she's not writing she's usually spouting off sarcastic remarks while drinking wine out of a coffee mug to look like a functional adult while chasing down her toddlers. She enjoys spending time with her family, watching reruns of FRIENDS, and the 24/7 flow of coffee that can be found in her veins. Be sure to follow her on social media for updates on what she's working on.

You can find her here:

Facebook: https://www.facebook.com/AuthorSamanthaBaca

Instagram: https://instagram.com/author_samantha_baca

Goodreads: http://www.goodreads.com/authorsamanthabaca

Facebook Reader Group:
https://www.facebook.com/groups/2945710968775398/

Webpage: https://authorsamanthabaca.wordpress.com

Newsletter: http://eepurl.com/g0NcSj

Other Books By Samantha Baca

'Til Death Do Us Part (Haven Brook Book 1)
https://www.amazon.com/dp/B087TG2JZV

The Cradle Will Fall (Haven Brook Book 2)
https://www.amazon.com/dp/B08GBZG3HS

The Ties That Bind (Haven Brook Book 3)
https://www.amazon.com/dp/B08P989VWK

Five Steps Ahead (Dark Shadows Book 1)
http://www.amazon.com/dp/B08CMXGL9G

Finding Love In Apartment 2C
https://www.amazon.com/dp/B08JHBFQH8